The Weight Of Destiny

A misfits Novel

By

Nyrae Dawn

Published by

Nyrae Dawn

Cover Design by X-Potion Designs

Edited by Sirena Van Schaik

Formatted by Angel's Indie Formatting

ISBN-13: 978-0990924319

"*The Weight of Destiny* unfolds like a storm. It is dark and electric and incredibly romantic. I lost and found myself. The characters are so vivid, so alive, you'll forget anything but them exists." **~ David James author of Between the Stars and Sky**

"Whenever I read Nyrae Dawn, I am reminded that words are her art, and she wields her paintbrush with all the skill of Rembrandt. The tender romance of Ryder and Virginia is palpable on the page, and the story sings with all the complexities of the interwoven plot. I read late into the night to finish this one, and once again, Nyrae has managed a masterpiece. LOVED." **~ USA Today and New York Times Bestselling Author Courtney Cole**

"*The Weight of Destiny* is art at its best, Ryder and Virginia canvasses on which the good and bad of life and love unfold in brilliant, true color." **~ Author Jamie Manning**

"*The Weight of Destiny* is YA at its absolute finest. Nyrae Dawn flawlessly brought two seemingly broken characters to life and showed everyone deserves a second chance at love and life. This breathtaking storytelling will blow you away." **~ USA Today Bestselling Author Tiffany King**

"Nyrae Dawn has once again given us characters that are so real we can't help but root for them. It's not just the growing romance between Ryder and Virginia, which is sweet and tender but also their complex relationships with family and friends that gives this story depth." **~ Heather Young-Nichols author of Up for Grabs**

Dedication

To Julie Prestsater. You are the kind of friend who has the ability to make me do things I never thought I would do. You remind me that it's okay to be silly and have fun. You make sure I reach my laugh quota every time we're together. Thank you for luring me out of my shell every once in a while. I'm blessed to call you my friend.

Prologue

Ryder

I touch the two wires together and see the spark. The car stutters but doesn't start so I do it again. Second time's a fucking charm. The engine purrs to life.

Clutch in. First gear. And then I'm out of here. My heart goes a million miles an hour as the car flies down the street. It's not fear shooting through my veins.

It's pride.

I think I hotwired that car even faster than Dad used to. He'll be stoked when I find him and tell him. Fourteen years old, and I'm better than the old man is.

I hardly slow down as I take a quick left.

Adrenaline still pumps through me. Dad used to tell me about the rush he'd get from taking shit. Tell me how it was the best feeling in the world, though I never got it—not until I started doing it myself.

My gloved thumbs drum on the steering wheel as I drive. My eyes don't stop darting left, right, forward, backward; whatever direction they can, hoping I don't see flashing blue and red lights. Hell, I don't want to see *any* headlights. Not until I can get as far away from this place as possible.

When I hit another intersection, I go right, heading straight for the freeway, still trying to figure out what direction I want to go in. I doubt Dad would have stayed in California. Not after all the shit he's gotten into here. He's from back East. Chicago. He's got a brother out there, and I wonder if he would have gone to see him?

Quickly, I scratch that idea. He wouldn't go to a family member's house. Not when he's got a warrant out for his arrest. But that doesn't mean he wouldn't go to Chicago. He always told me how much he missed it out there. It also doesn't mean my uncle won't know where to find him.

It's my best bet, and sure as hell better than staying here with my older brother, who wants nothing to do with me. Not that I want anything to do with him, either. It's been that way since Dad left us boys to fend for ourselves.

I glance down at the gas gauge. There's about half a tank, which isn't too bad. Once I put enough distance between myself and home, I'll find a car to syphon from.

Never pay for anything if you don't have to. That was one of Dad's first lessons.

There's a shit ton of food in the backseat, hoses for gas, and I know I'll have no problem getting whatever else I need.

I drum my thumbs faster, rock a little as I go, trying to calm the excitement blowing up my insides.

I'm good at this. I love being good at it.

For about an hour, I'm flying. Living. Hopeful. I'm going to get out of this place. Going to find Dad, and do the things we do best. I'm going to *live*.

When the car swerves to the right, I can hardly keep control of it. Jerking the wheel, I try and compensate for the momentum of the blown tire only I pull too far. It doesn't matter when I attempt to go the opposite direction. There's not enough time, and the front of the car slams into the guardrail.

The airbag explodes in my face, shooting pain through my nose. Smoke billows out of the hood. "Shit!" Over and over, I slam my hands into the steering wheel. The pain in my face doesn't matter. I screwed up. My chance at finding Dad has been blown, and if I don't get out of here, I'll get arrested for the second time since he's been gone.

Again, I'm stuck here.

Shoving the door open, I stumble out of the car, grab my shit, and get the hell out of dodge.

Chapter One

Virginia

There once was a girl named Perfect with hair made of honey and a life made of dreams. No one knew it was all a lie. Perfect wasn't perfect. Her life wasn't either, but as long as everyone believed, she made herself think she could too.

Ernest Hemingway suffered from depression. He ended his own life by shooting himself.

Sylvia Plath was severely depressed as well. She stuck her head in the oven and poisoned herself with carbon monoxide.

Annette Klinger committed suicide, too. Most people don't know who she is, but she was also a writer. She was my grandmother. When Mom was thirteen, Annette left her. Three years later, Mom found out Annette hung herself a year and a half after leaving.

Mom's a writer too.

When I was five, Mom told me Virginia Woolf was one of her favorite authors. She couldn't wait until I was old enough to read about Mrs. Dalloway.

I thought it was so cool that she named me after Virginia Woolf. Mom was this bright light: fun and exciting. Sometimes, it was as though she was a kid just like me. I couldn't believe she named *me* after someone who was her favorite. It made me feel fun and exciting like her.

When I went to bed the night she told me about her favorite author, she tucked me in, pushed my hair out of my face, and then asked if I wanted to know more about Virginia Woolf. Before I could reply, she told me Virginia was sad. She'd been so sad that one day she stuffed her pockets full of rocks to weigh herself down and stepped into a river.

It wasn't the kind of bedtime story I'd been looking for.

That's when I knew, as alive as Mom was, she was different as well. It's when I first started to fear I would grow up to be different like her. No, Mom wasn't typically depressed as so many of those greats were, but she's always had her own demons.

When I got older, I made a conscious decision not to let that happen to me.

That brings me to today as I watch Mom's arms flail while she excitedly screams at my principal so sharply it makes my head ring. All I can think is that I have a writer mom who's never been stable. A mom who is wild, and reckless, and has other people who live inside her head. How she had a writer mom who was also wild and reckless. And how Mom chose to name me after an author who drowned herself.

Is it just me or does that seem a little like tempting fate?

No, not me. I will not be like this.

"Mrs. Nichols, I'm going to need you to lower your voice," Principal Toms tells her.

"*Ms.* It's Ms. My husband and I are separated, and I'm not yelling. Am I yelling? I just have this really great idea and I want Virginia to help me with it."

My face burns as whispers start behind me and people from my school witness Freak Out 101, Charity Nichols-style—*the* Charity Nichols, because everyone knows who she is. New York Times and USA Today bestselling author and all.

I've done so well keeping the wild part of my life a secret. It's not like Mom is this way all the time. She hasn't been like this in years. But then it hits me...what if she's not my mom right now?

No. They fixed that. She's better. She has to be.

"It's fine. I can go." I step forward, willing to do anything to get out of here. To get *her* out of here before more people show up. Oh God, what will they think? Quickly, I scan the crowd to see if my best friends Jamie and Hailey are around.

"Lulu, you can't go. You're not allowed to check out unless your dad approves it," Mr. Toms says.

Obviously, there's a reason for that.

"But I'm her *mom*." She flits around, unable to stay still. I exhale a deep breath. She said she's my mom. That means she's still her.

It shocks me that she didn't freak when he called me Lulu. She sometimes does when she's like this, even though she's the only one who doesn't call me by my middle name.

"I'm her *MOM!*" she says again, each word getting louder.

Mom pushes her light brown hair out of her face. It's the same color as mine. We look almost exactly alike. More like sisters, most people say. Her mom looked like us too, and for the millionth time, I wonder if Grandma had different people living inside her. Maybe Sylvia, Ernest, or Virginia Woolf did as well.

"Ms. Nichols, it's the rules. I'm sorry—"

"Mom," I cut the principal off. She turns to me, more people filling in around us. Of course she had to come between classes. Jamie's here now, which means Hailey must be close. My feet itch to carry me away so badly; I want to run so I don't have to deal with this. She hasn't had an outburst in so long. Why is she having one now?

"Virginia, I'm so excited. I got this great idea. I was thinking we could go on a road trip. I want to paint the ocean. I want to write a story about the ocean, and you know how important it is for me to experience what I'm working on. Not around here, though. I'm thinking Oregon. We can stop by your house and grab a bag. It'll be a blast, don't you think?"

She sounds younger than me, giddy excitement bouncing around inside her. It's like she can't control her body. Everything's magnified. A million-watt smile, a loud, excited voice, her body a jittery mess.

It reminds me of how she used to be at times. It wasn't until later that I found out why.

Oh God, don't let this ever be me. I don't want this to be me.

"Lulu?" Hailey's voice sounds from beside me, confused.

I shake my head at her, pleading with my eyes for her to step back, for her, and everyone else, to somehow unsee what's going on.

"I have a huge test tomorrow, Mom. I…I can't. What about this weekend? Then Dad can arrange it so I don't have to come to school next week. We'll have more time that way."

The whispers get louder. Mom moves around like a druggie too high to keep still.

"Charity, she can't go today. Why don't you come with me and we'll plan the trip." It's Dad's voice behind me, and I realize someone from school must have called him.

Immediately, I exhale a sigh of relief. Dad's here. Even though they've been separated for years now, Dad can handle her. He makes her better.

"Dave! You're here! Finally. I want to take Virginia to Oregon. Do you want to go with us? It can be like old times. We can get a tent and camp right there by the water."

"Lulu can't today. She has a test. Why don't we go outside and pick another day?" Dad gives me a sad smile as he wraps an arm around Mom's shoulders, leading her out of the school's commons area.

My heart is going wild, probably like Mom's is doing, except it's not because I'm excited. *You can handle this. You're Lulu Nichols. You always have things under control.*

Taking a deep breath, I look at Hailey and Jamie, then smile. "You guys ready to go to class?"

"Umm… Lu?" Jamie pushes one of her braids behind her ear. She has a million of them in her hair. She always does. I wish I could get away with that, but it wouldn't look as good on me as it does against her dark skin.

"Alright everyone, get to class. Teachers will be giving detention to anyone who is late." *Thank you,* I want to tell Mr. Toms as he tries to disperse the crowd.

"We better go. We're going to be late." I've never had detention in my life and I definitely don't plan to start now.

Hailey grabs my arm. She has the blondest hair in the world. Sometimes we call her Halo. "Lulu… your mom…" It's not like they've never met Mom before, but they've never seen the truth.

They only know the persona I try to create.

And I'm so totally not doing this. Not now, not ever. I worked hard for my reputation, and I don't plan on letting it go down the drain. *"Fine.* If you guys want to be late, go for it. I'm not screwing up my perfect attendance for nothing."

Pulling out of Hailey's grasp, I walk away. I manage to avoid them the rest of the day. It's not so easy after school. We have a Future Business Leaders of America meeting. I usually love FBLA, but today, I can't focus. For the first time ever, I fake a stomach ache and cut out early. Dad's called my cell a million times. For hours, I drive around, until it hits me what I'm doing. I'd give just about anything not to go home right now, but that's not how I work.

Logic. I go through life based on logic, and putting things off doesn't change anything.

After turning my Prius around, I drive home, determined to work with Dad on coming up with a plan so nothing like this happens again.

Chapter Two

Ryder

Like usual, my brother is fucking trippin'.

And not the good kind, either.

"It's one day, Luke. It's not that big a deal. Why do you give a shit if I go to school or not?"

Luke rolls his eyes. "I'm going to pretend you didn't ask me that, Ry. You do realize if you screw up too much, they can take you away from me, right?"

He's been threatening me with that ever since Dad went into hiding when I was fourteen. I'm pretty sure it's wishful thinking because no one seems to give a flying fuck what I do, except for Luke. (Besides the cops, but they care more about the stealing than school.) Everyone who knows Luke sees that he would rather be anywhere other than here with me.

Luke had a plan. Luke was better than all of us. Luke's ass got stuck with me.

It's not like Dad isn't coming home, though. He'll come back for me when I turn eighteen. He told me he'd always come back for me. It's the only thing keeping me here. I've talked to him once since he bailed—after the second time I got arrested for stealing. Not the car; they were never able to nail that one on me. But when Dad got in touch, he said I needed to keep my nose clean. If I get locked up, he won't be able to come back for me. It's hard as hell, but I'd rather play the good boy than risk not going with him.

Then we'll all be happy. I'll be with Dad, doing what we love, and Luke would be free of me—after he played savior.

"I'm seventeen. Do you really think they would waste their time taking me away when I'm almost legal to be on my own anyway?" I kick back on my bed and put my feet up.

"Why don't you repeat the part of that sentence where you say how old you are? You're almost eighteen. Don't you think you should stop wasting time and get your shit together? You graduate this year, man. You have your whole life ahead of you. Don't fuck it up like Dad did."

Aaaand...time to go. I hate it when he gets all self-righteous like this. "You seem to forget we can't all be as good as you, Luke. And maybe you shouldn't talk shit about someone who isn't here to defend himself. He's our *dad.*" I push off the bed and stand up. The guy raised us. He always made sure Luke and I had food to eat, no matter how he had to get it. I respect that. He did what had to be done.

Luke rolls his eyes. His hair is getting a little longer, the dark strands going into his narrow, blue eyes. "I would say it to his face, but he left us, Ry. Remember that. He doesn't deserve your loyalty. He's a liar and a thief. He's a criminal, and not because he loved us so much he wanted to take care of us, but because he loved stealing *more* than he did us."

I ball my hands into fists, wanting nothing more than to knock my brother out. It would serve him right. I get this little twitch in the right side of my forehead when I feel like I'm going to explode.

Luke forgets *he's* the one who left first. The second he graduated high school he was out of here, and he didn't look back once until Dad had to bail. Dad had no choice in leaving. Luke did. While he was off pretending he was better than the rest of us, Dad kept teaching me how to survive. He taught me how to get whatever I need so I'll never have to work shitty jobs only to still be broke, the way Luke does. Dad taught me how to be a man.

"Shit, Ry." Luke shakes his head. "You're going to be just like him if you're not careful. He's a loser. He's nothing. Two strikes, bro. You have two strikes already. One more and you're going to juvie for more than a couple days like last time. It's not much longer until they'll try you as an adult. You don't get it, but—"

"I'd rather be like him than a sellout like you." It's not like Luke really gives a shit anyway. He cares that he can't be at his rich-kid college, and that's about it. "I'm out."

Without another word, I walk from my room.

I don't have a car, and the thought of stealing Luke's just to piss him off lands in my brain. It would serve him right. But I know he'll call the cops on me and then I'll be screwed, so I call my best friend, Shane, as I walk from the house.

"We're right up the road, man. Be right there," he says before I hang up.

I walk down the street so I don't have to wait at home. Luke is like an annoying cold sometimes, and I can't get rid of him no matter what I do. What's his problem anyway? We were lucky. Hell, most of my friends don't have dads, but we did. Ours wanted to be around. He taught us the kind of lessons you don't learn in school. The kind of stuff you need.

Yeah, a lot of it wasn't on the up and up, but no one will ever be able to say I don't know how to take care of myself.

I can pick a lock in under twenty-five seconds.

I can hotwire a car just as quickly.

In no time at all, I can come up with a story to get what I want. I can get out of detention when I feel like putting in the effort, or I can talk a waitress into a free meal by making her believe I lost my wallet.

In other words, things I can actually use. Not algebra, and shit that Luke thinks is so important.

Hoooonk!

I jump and then shake my head as Shane pulls his car up next to me. I lean into the open passenger window. It's pretty much full, which I should have known it would be. Tanner and his boyfriend Cody are in the back. Tanner's leaning against Cody, taking up two seats. Cody's messing with Tanner's Mohawk, and Tanner winks at me.

"Luke givin' you shit?" Tan asks.

Totally not going there, so I ignore him and look at Drea in the passenger seat. She's gorgeous. Everyone sees it and she knows it. She's got smooth, light brown skin and big, round eyes. A couple months ago she got a Marilyn Monroe piercing, which I'm pretty sure was made just for her. She's the kind of girl who doesn't screw around. When I first met her, I didn't pronounce her name right—it's "Drey-uh"—and I thought she would knock me out. I like that about her. "I'm sitting with you."

Shane has an old Cadillac with a bench seat in front. Drea smiles and scoots over as I open the door.

"What up, man?" Shane asks.

Getting in, I close the door behind me. "Nothin'."

Drea's long, dark hair is over her shoulder. It brushes my arm, she's sitting so close to me. We've fucked around before. Probably will again. But we've always been cool like that. We get together when we want to have a good time, and that's the end of it. People who don't know her give her hell sometimes, but we take care of it for Drea. There's nothing wrong with a girl who likes sex.

"Where were you guys going?" I ask as Shane pulls away. I finger the snakebite piercings in my bottom lip.

"Hoping to chill at your house, but obviously that's a no-go." Shane glances at me.

Automatically, I tense up. Fucking Luke. I'm still pissed at him.

Tanner leans forward. I feel his breath on my neck so I turn to see him looking at me. "You cool?"

Tanner's good about that—not that I want him in my business right now—but he's always the one who will make sure everyone is okay instead of just letting things slide.

"Yep. Luke's being a douchebag is all." You'd think living with your twenty-two year old brother would be cool. Not when it's mine, though.

Tanner leans backward with Cody again. We drive around for a while before pulling over by this quiet stretch of ocean. We live in a crappy town outside of San Francisco—far enough from the city to feel like the middle of nowhere, but close enough that some of the rich people who work in the city live in the town next to us and drive downtown for work.

Shane pulls out his pipe. We hotbox the car before the five of us get out and head toward the water. Cody builds a fire in one of the fire pits. It's dead down here. It's only September but the evenings are already pretty cold.

We stay here as it gets dark, talking crap and hanging out. Luke thinks my friends are shit, just like he thinks I am, but I feel more at home with these guys than I do him.

It doesn't take long until Drea starts kissing my neck. Shane looks over at us. "When's the wedding?"

"Funny."

Tanner and Cody are in their own world. Tan is on Cody's lap whispering something in his ear. They're always whispering stuff back and forth. I turn toward Drea and kiss her back, thinking she's the perfect distraction I need tonight, and knowing all I am is a distraction for her, too.

Chapter Three

Virginia

When I get home after driving around, I'm not surprised to see Mom sitting at our dining room table with Dad.

The table means they want to talk. It's not that Dad and I don't eat there together every night we're home. We do. But every important conversation the three of us have also takes place there.

When we lived together and had family meetings, this is where we'd sit. The only difference was back then the table sat at Mom's house in the city. It's where we talked when Mom had problems and we needed to come up with a plan. It's where we cried when they announced they were getting separated. And even though I know it's important that we talk about today, I'm avoiding that stupid table at all costs. I can't do this with Mom here. It's easier when it's just Dad.

"Lulu," Dad says at the same time Mom mutters, "Virginia."

"Virginia," Dad corrects himself as Mom adds, "Lulu," and then they both look at each other and laugh.

There's a little voice inside my head that tells me it's funny, that I should laugh with them, but all I can think about is the fact that Mom called me Lulu. That means this is serious. There's definitely no way I'm sitting at that table now.

"The showers weren't working today after PE." Truth. "I need to shower before I can do anything." Lie.

Dad sighs. "Lulu," he says again.

Turning, I face them while walking backward toward the stairs. "I'm serious! Don't worry. I'm already working with the student council on what we can do to make sure the showers get fixed quickly." And then, before they can try and force me to the table, I run upstairs.

I swear, I hardly get the door closed before it's getting shoved open again. Mom. She pushes way more than Dad does. If she wasn't here, he would have waited downstairs for me.

"Mom! This is my room. You can't just come in." The whininess in my voice is annoying, but I'm hoping it will do the trick.

I fall to my bed, and she keeps coming. She has a sad smile on her face that I hate to see there. I love it when she's happy. I used to want to be just like her.

Mom pushes a lock of her honey-brown hair behind her ear and sits beside me. Before I know it, Dad is here with her.

"I am so sorry, Virginia." Her arm raises and she does the same thing with my matching hair that she just did with her own. It makes tears spring to my eyes but I hold them back before they can slip free.

The urge to stick my fingers into my ears and start humming hits me. If I can't hear what she has to say, then I can pretend it's not true. I can pretend I have normal parents who get separated and hate each other, instead of a mom who isn't always my mom.

"I've been…going through some things lately. I'm still seeing my psychiatrist, but…" Mom's words trail off.

Thank you. Don't say them. Go home and let me go sit in Dad's office with him. We can talk statistics and rules because those things clear both our heads.

"Go on, Charity." Dad grabs her hand, and suddenly anger teases me, burned edges on a piece of paper. Why does he want to hear this? Why is he making her tell me? How can he be so understanding when I can't?

Mom takes a deep breath, her eyes flooded pools. "You know I worked really hard with my doctor for a long time."

Crossing my arms, I speak. "Just say it, Mom." The sooner she does, the sooner I can try to forget it.

"There's a new personality. It doesn't seem to be very bad, and unlike the others, she accepts who I am. She knows I'm your mom, and we have no doubt that we can integrate her as well."

New personality, new personality, new personality. How many people can say their mom used to have more than one person living inside them? That besides being Charity the mom and the author, she also used to be Robin the rebellious teenage girl who wanted to be my friend, and Samantha the person who hated me?

When I was in the third grade, girls at my school were picking on me. They called me names and made me cry, and the only person I wanted was my mom. I ran into the house when I got off the school bus and wrapped my arms around her legs. I was surprised when she didn't hold me back so I looked up at her through a blur.

"Mommy?" I'd said.

She rolled her eyes. "Ugh. It's you again."

That was when I knew I would never be able to depend on her. That was when I decided I wouldn't depend on anyone.

It wasn't her fault, I got that, but I was the one who felt my heart breaking apart. I was the only one who could fix it too. So I had. Just like I will now.

"Who is it?" I ask, not letting my emotions weigh me down.

Another sigh from Mom. "Her name is Amelia. She's not like Samantha. She loves you. We came close to some…revelations in therapy. That's when Amelia showed up. I'm going to do everything I can to fix this. We'll do what we can to integrate so this won't happen again."

Amelia loves me so much she embarrassed me in front of half the school? No thank you. I don't tell them how I feel, though. I listen while Mom talks about therapy. Dad's there to support her, and her psychiatrist is hopeful. They go on and on, but their voices just get farther and farther away.

Why does it have to be this way? Why can't she just be my mom?

I snap out of it when Mom says, "They're blank. You're not writing?" She fingers one of the journals beside my bed.

Mom is obviously big on writing since it's what she does for a living, but she's always pushing it on me as well. *Writing your feelings is therapeutic* and *you're so talented, Virginia.* I don't want to be talented. Sylvia Plath was talented, as was Virginia Woolf. Just like Mom is. Writing is the last thing I want to do.

It sets my insides aflame again. It makes no sense that she thinks I would want to be like her and Grandma. Why would I want to embrace that creative side she's always saying is so important when I've seen what it's done?

I don't want to be like the writers Mom loves. I don't want to

23

abandon my daughter and then end my life like Grandma did. I don't want to not be myself like the famous Charity Nichols.

"I have to go." Standing, I grab my keys from the bedside table.

"Lulu." Dad reaches for me but Mom grabs his arm.

"Let her go, Dave."

He nods, and I leave. The whole time I'm driving, I fight back tears. I drive out of town, until I realize I'm in Henderson. It's not the safest place but I don't care.

The sound of the ocean flows through my lowered window. Water isn't really my favorite thing but still I pull over. It's so big out here, it's easy to get lost. To pretend things aren't going to fall apart again.

Chapter Four

Ryder

It's not long after Drea and I stop making out that a few more people we know show up. They're pretty cool, and they have beer with them, which everyone is stoked about.

Shane doesn't drink. It's not his thing, but I can tell by his jittery movements that he's excited to have a few more people to chill with us. It's not hard to tell when Shane is pumped about something because he can't stop moving around. If we weren't at the beach, he'd be riding his skateboard. He kicks ass on that thing.

Glancing over at Cody, I see him move the backpack he always has with him. It's no doubt full of spray paint. He paints some pretty badass pictures in all sorts of places where he's not supposed to. He must be ready to go find a place to paint.

Everyone talks and laughs and I try to join in. I'm as down for a good time as the next guy, but tonight, I'm just not feeling it.

He left us, Ry...

He doesn't deserve your loyalty...

He's a criminal, and not because he loved us so much he wanted to take care of us, but because he loved stealing more than he did us.

Screw Luke for putting shit like that in my head. Dad and me were like partners. Dad wanted me around.

Pushing to my feet, I dust sand the sand off. "I'm going for a walk."

Drea looks up at me, her eyes searching for something. "Want me to go with you?"

"Nah, it's cool." I ruffle her hair and she laughs. She's the only girl I could imagine doing something like that with—and she needs this, the closeness our group provides, because she sure as shit doesn't get it at home. "Give these guys hell while I'm gone." I nod toward all the bodies sitting around the fire and she turns her attention back to them.

I walk for what feels like forever, until I can't see the glow of the fire in the distance or hear the laughter of my friends. There's an old dock up ahead. It's blocked off by poles, metal, and signs because it's falling apart. It's from when smaller boats used to come to this stretch of beach, but it hasn't been used in forever.

Deciding this is as good a place as any, I sit on the sand, nothing but black ocean in front of me. Is Dad somewhere by the sea? He used to love it. Before Luke decided he was too good for us, Dad used to take us to the ocean all the time.

Movement by the water catches my eyes. There's a flash of white, a shirt I guess, as someone stands and looks toward the dock.

The person looks little, and I'm pretty sure it's a girl. She doesn't stay in the same spot for very long before she starts moving for the dock, using her phone for a flashlight.

"What the fuck are you doing?" I whisper to myself as I watch her.

She pauses for a second before she starts to climb through the open spaces on the cheap "wall" they put up. Then, she gets onto the old wood. Before I realize what I'm doing, I push to my feet.

She crawls under some extra ropes they have there for protection. "Hey!" I call out but she keeps going. It's hard to tell from this far, but it looks like the water is licking at the platform of the dock each time another wave comes in.

This twitchy feeling lands in my chest. I'm not sure what it is, but then my feet automatically start moving forward; first slow, and then faster, toward her. "Hey! What are you doing?" I yell again. As soon as the words leave my lips, she looks my way then screams as her arms fly up.

I'm running now even though I can't tell what's going on. I see her sink lower and scream again right before another wave rolls in, this one splashing over her.

"Holy shit." I'm not a real track-star kind of guy, but I can push my ass when I need to. Another wave comes up, slamming into her. The closer I get I can tell she's trying to scramble up, but something's stopping her.

Another wave hits as I skid to a stop in front of the dock. Like she did, I push my way through the barrier. I think her foot went through the wood, and she's stuck. She looks older than I originally thought. Closer to my age, but she has a small frame.

I grab the dock and pull myself up.

"The wood is weak…" she warns. And I'm bigger than she is… I get what she's saying. Her voice is shaky as hell.

"No shit." My legs tremble a little as I ease toward her. Water pools at my ankles. *Don't fucking break. Please don't collapse.*

"Be careful," she says.

It only takes me a few steps to reach her. The wood bends beneath my feet as I lean forward to grab her. "Are you cut or anything?"

The light from her phone shines on her as she shakes her head. The first thing I notice is how wide and green her eyes are, and, stupidly, I wonder if they're always that big or just because she's scared to death.

"Put your arms around my neck." She does. I wrap mine around her and pull her out. She's shivering and soaking wet. "You're cool. I got you." The words come out automatically, when I really want to ask her what the hell she was thinking.

I manage to get her free, just as more water comes in. I'm wet from the knees down. The wood bows with each step I take, old screws and bolts giving way. My heart is going crazy, a wild drumbeat.

The second I step into the sand, far enough away that the water doesn't touch us, I let out a deep breath, and set her down.

And then I'm pissed. "What the fuck was that? Are you trying to kill yourself?"

The moon is bright tonight, shining down on her. The fear in her eyes warps into something else. Anger, maybe? "What? No! I would never do that. I just..." She looks down. "I just wanted to go out there..."

"And the fact that it was closed off didn't clue you in that it's not safe?"

"Maybe that was the point," she mumbles, whatever that means.

"So you weren't trying to kill yourself, but the fact that it wasn't safe was your point? What are you, some kind of adrenaline junkie?" Yeah, right. Totally doesn't fit, but whatever her reason, maybe next time she should look for her high where she doesn't chance someone stumbling upon her and risking themselves.

"Yeah, obviously. That's me, Lulu the adrenaline junkie. Next time, I'm jumping out of a plane. Do you want to come along?"

I cross my arms, amused for some reason. "You're not very grateful to someone who just saved your life." My eyes travel down on autopilot. "Your shirt's wet. Nice bra."

Her eyes go big again, and I can tell I've scandalized her. This girl definitely isn't looking for some kind of high. She's not from around here, either.

Arms on her chest, she whips around. I don't need to see her face to know she's embarrassed. What's the big deal? It's just a bra. No different than a bikini top. I can't imagine Drea or any of the girls I know freaking out over that. The urge to laugh hits me, but the shake of her shoulders stops me.

Is she crying?

Fuck.

"I'm not going to hurt you. I just saved your life. Here…" And then, before I know what I'm doing, I'm pulling my hoodie off and handing it to her. She turns just enough to see it. She grabs the sweatshirt before jerking it over her head.

It drowns her as she turns to me again; her face nothing but those big, green eyes that are now tinted red. Her whole body is trembling, her long, light-brown hair soaking. One look at her tells me she's a rich kid. It's obvious by her clothes and the way she holds herself.

This is the kind of girl Dad would latch on to. The kind he would trick into giving him what he wanted. She looks like a raccoon, with make-up around her eyes, but somehow I know she's the kind of girl with a whole group of rich-kid friends. Straight A's, student council president, or whatever it's called…but there's something else there, too. Tonight, I think she might be the loneliest girl in the world.

It's that last thought that makes me shove ideas of what Dad would do out of my head.

"Go home. You don't belong out here. Warm up, call your friends, write in your diary or whatever you do when you have a bad day. Your world will be perfect again in the morning."

Her eyes get huge with shock, but whatever. Turning, I start back toward my friends. I'm no more than ten feet away when she speaks. Her voice is steadier than it has been since I saved her when she calls out over the sound of the waves, "No."

Chapter Five

Virginia

There once was a girl named Fear. Everything scared her, but she couldn't let anyone know. Maybe if she fought hard enough, she could change her name to Strength. That's who she wanted to be.

~*~

The guy with the piercings in his bottom lip stops, but doesn't turn. His pants are baggy, like guys wear. Not the guys at my school, because they'd get kicked out—and honestly, they probably wouldn't want to anyway. He runs a hand through his messy hair. I shouldn't have told him no. I should have just let him go and done my own thing. I know he saved me, but that doesn't mean he gets to tell me what to do. "And thank you. For saving me, I mean."

At that, he turns around. His eyebrows are pulled together, as though he's never had someone thank him before. He has this cockiness to him that makes me hate him on principle, but this edge that makes me take a step backward, too.

"It's only polite that I say thank you. You *did* save me." Ugh. What had I been thinking climbing out there? I can't believe I did that. It was reckless and stupid. I don't do things that are

31

reckless and stupid. I'd just wanted…I don't even know what I wanted. Whatever it was, it wasn't to get trapped and almost drown.

"You're not going to go home, are you?" pierced-lip boy asks.

Definitely not. Dad would freak if I came home wet like this, wearing a guy's sweatshirt, and I obviously don't want anyone to know I did something so ridiculous and crazy. It's something Mom would do, climb out there to get a better view. So she could write or draw there. Mom wouldn't think of the consequences, just like I hadn't, whether she was really Mom at the time or not.

Oh God. I could have drowned. Walking out there was almost like putting rocks in my pocket. Fear grips my throat like an old, scarred, gnarled hand. I could have drowned, just like Virginia Woolf!

Get it together, Lulu. You're fine. Don't let him see you freaking out. "No, but it's just the beach. I'll be fine."

Cockily, he quirks a brow at me.

"I'm not stupid. I'm not going to go out there again. I'm going to sit here and dry off. You can go, though I don't know how I'll get you your hoodie back. I guess I should give it to you now." Then I'll sit here and freeze in a see-thru shirt. Maybe I should just go home. The thought makes a heavy rock land in my stomach.

Pierced-lip boy sighs. I begrudgingly notice that he's kind of cute in a bad-boy way. It doesn't make me feel any more comfortable around him, though. "Keep the hoodie. My friends have a bonfire up the beach. You can come chill with us and get warm, have a beer or something."

Automatically, I shake my head. I am not going to sit with a bunch of strangers while they get drunk and he tells them about what I did. I want to forget it ever happened, not look like a lunatic.

"I promise, we don't bite. Well, sometimes Tanner and Cody bite each other, and Drea's...yeah she's not totally safe, either. Most girls *want* Shane to bite them, but he's pretty picky about the girls he hooks up with. Not that he wouldn't choose you, he just doesn't choose anyone that often."

Whoa. I'm sort of at a loss for words, not sure how to reply to that. "This is the part where you try to scare me into going home, right? Why don't we skip it? You go your way and I'll go mine."

Fighting my smile, I look away, proud of myself. That sounded way more believable than I thought it would, because honestly, the thought of hanging out with his friends does make me nervous.

"Woulda' got me if you didn't smile and look away. It's okay to be freaked. You never know how us kids from the wrong side of the tracks can be." Then he does the strangest thing: he sits down in the sand, half his pants wet and all. "You're not scared of me, too, are you? Aren't you supposed to see me as your knight in shining armor now or something?"

I roll my eyes.

"That's obviously what you're looking for. You saved me out there, and now you have to protect the poor, little girl so no bad guys get her while she sits on the beach. I don't need anyone to save me."

"Nah, you got me wrong, rich girl. I'm nobody's savior. I know who and what I am, and I'm proud of it. Have fun." He stands again and starts to walk away. His voice plays in my head. The way it caught when he spoke. Guilt starts snaking it's way through my insides. Yeah, he was a jerk to me and he's a little

33

scary, but he *did* save me. And he gave me his hoodie. He didn't have to do either of those things.

As much as I hate to admit it, I don't want to be alone. I want to pretend today didn't happen, the same way I pretend my past didn't happen.

"Wait," jumps out of my mouth before I can stop it. Saying it, feeling it, makes me raw, exposed in a way that makes my skin itch. Needing is weak, and I promised myself I would never be that. If I'm weak, it will be easier for our family curse to get its claws into me.

Pierced-lip boy stops, pauses, and then turns around. He's way taller than me. His hair dark, and sort of wavy. He doesn't say a word until he gets back over to me. "You should take your pants off."

"I…What…I'm not…"

He laughs and shakes his head. "I'm not trying to have sex with you. Unless you want to, then I'm game."

My cheeks get hot next. I've had boyfriends, but no one has ever said something like that to me before.

"You're shivering, and the wet clothes make it worse. Take your pants off. You're small enough to sit with your knees in the hoodie to keep you warm."

Oh. Okay. I guess that makes sense. "Turn around."

"Really?" There's enough question in his tone that tells me he's not asking to be a jerk. He's genuinely surprised I would ask him that. "It's not like I'm going to attack you."

Still, he turns around. As fast as I can, I slip out of my pants, lay them out and then sit down. I pull my knees up into the hoodie like he said, immediately feeling warmer. "Okay, you can turn around now."

He does, and then he sits beside me. We're quiet for a few minutes, and again I feel my cheeks warm. Why did I ask him to stay? I don't even know this guy. I don't need anyone.

"You can go," I whisper.

"Nah, it's cool. I didn't really feel like being around a bunch of people tonight anyway."

We go back to being quiet again. Pierced-lip boy rolls his pant legs up, and then stares out at the ocean. Questions rapid-fire in my brain: why doesn't he want to be around people? Is he as lonely as he looks?

And then something strange happens... I start to pretend he's like me. That he feels cursed to be who his parents are. That he's trapped. That he lives a lie, with everyone close to him because he's so scared to show them who he is.

Because he's afraid of what that might be.

I open my mouth to say something, I don't know what, but his phone rings, saving me.

He pulls it out of his pocket and answers with a, "What's up?"

He covers the cell and looks at me. "Do you have a car?"

I nod.

Back on the phone, he says, "Nah, I'm cool. I have a ride. I'll catch you guys later."

I don't bring up the fact that he didn't ask me or that I don't know where he lives. I'm just thankful not to be alone tonight. Not to have to think about Mom, Dad...or Amelia.

"Your name's Lulu?" He asks after a bit.

Immediately I tense up. Reaching over, I touch my jeans to make sure my keys, with my mini pepper spray on them, are still in the pocket.

"Relax. I'm not stalking you. You said it earlier."

Oh yeah. Duh. Little flashes of Mom from today flitter into my head. How excited she looked at the school, how sad she looked at my house. "My mom named me after Virginia Woolf." I'm not sure why I say this. "But my middle name is Lulu. That's what I go by."

Pierced-lip boy nods.

More quiet, so much quiet I wonder if he feels like he's suffocating on it like I am.

"So I guess this means you don't want to have sex?" There's laughter in his voice, and before I know it, I'm laughing as well. I'm not choking on the quiet anymore so when we slip back into it, I feel strangely okay.

Chapter Six

Ryder

I'm a good boy all week, just like Luke wants me to be. I go to school every day so I don't have to hear him bitch. He spends most of his time at the diner he runs so we've managed to avoid each other pretty well.

It's Friday, and I'm planning on going out with my friends tonight. I'm broke and haven't gotten a new hoodie since I gave mine to Virginia. If I ever see her again, it would probably piss her off that I call her that, but I can't make myself call her Lulu. It sounds like something you name a poodle, not a good girl with big, green eyes.

She'd tried to give me the hoodie when she dropped me off at home, but I could tell she was still cold so I let her keep it. Her pants were still damp, but she hadn't liked my idea of driving without them.

Right as Luke walks into the room, I chuckle about her modesty.

"What are you laughing at?" He tucks his work shirt into his pants.

We've never done the "talking to each other" thing. I don't see why he thinks we'd start now. "Nothin'. Do you have twenty bucks I can borrow? I need a hoodie." My fingers tingle with the desire to just go take one. It's what Dad would tell me to do. Well, if I didn't have to keep out of trouble, he would.

Luke frowns. "What happened to yours?"

Dude. How hard is it to just say yes or no? "Never mind. I'll figure it out myself." Grabbing the remote, I click on the TV.

Luke walks over and rips it out of my hand and hits 'power'. "All I did was ask you a question. You had a hoodie and now it's gone. Geez, Ry. Why the hell are you always so pissed at me?"

I don't know, sticks in my head like peanut butter to the roof of a mouth.

Luke jerks his wallet out of his pocket, pulls out a twenty and drops it onto my lap. "Whatever. I need to finish getting ready for work."

Before I reply to him, he's walking into the bathroom and closing the door behind himself.

Fuck. Guilt washes the peanut butter away and takes its place. I know Luke. Whatever the reason I didn't have my hoodie, he would have given me twenty dollars for a new one. I didn't have to be a dick to him about it.

"Hey." The springs in the couch creak when I stand. It's old, like really old. We've needed a new one forever. I don't even think they put springs like that in couches anymore.

Just as I'm about to make it to the bathroom to…I don't know, thank him? I hear tires on gravel. Shane isn't supposed to be here for another couple hours, but it's not like Luke ever has anyone over, so it has to be him.

I make a quick turn, avoiding the hall bathroom, and go to the front door. I pull it open to see a little, red Prius idling in my driveway.

What the hell is she doing here? Quickly I close the door behind myself, as though that will make a difference. It was one thing to see my house at night, but another in the daytime. I can pretty much guarantee her place is probably five times the size of mine, and a whole lot nicer.

Not that I care about shit like that.

Jogging down the porch stairs, I head her way. She doesn't get out of the car until I make it to the driver's side door. The second she's out, I snap, "What are you doing here?"

She flinches, sending another dose of guilt through me. First Luke, now her.

Virginia recovers quickly, shoving my hoodie into my arms. "It's called manners. You lent me something, and I only thought it right that I return it. Maybe you can learn a lesson or two from it."

She rips her door open so quickly I have to jump back. There is no doubt in my mind that this girl will leave, and part of me wants to let her. It's not like we're ever going to be friends. She won't be like Drea is to me, or even just chill like Shane, Tanner and Cody. There's way too much shit going on in my life for me to worry about hurting some rich girl's feelings, but she didn't have to bring the hoodie back. Now, I won't have to keep the money from Luke. I hate taking money from him.

Dad always said never owe anyone anything, and it's a lesson I stick to.

Reaching out, I put an arm between her and the entrance so she can't get in. "Sorry. Shitty day." I hold up my sweatshirt. "Thanks for this." It smells totally different than it did when I gave it to her. Not that it was dirty, but it smells like girl mixed

39

with something fruity. It feels softer than it normally does as well.

"You washed it for me?" Maybe this shouldn't surprise me. I'm sure she did it more out of obligation than anything, but most people just don't do stuff like that for me.

"Yes. Have you ever heard of fabric softener? You should invest in some."

Her comment should piss me off, but I find myself smiling. "You're awfully sarcastic for a rich girl." I can see Drea saying something like that, but typically girls like Virginia look scared of my friends and I, instead of talking shit to us.

Virginia rolls her eyes. Damn, the girl is hot. Her hair is shinier than I'm used to. Not that it looks like it has stuff in it, but...hell, I don't know. It just glows. She's a little bit curvy. She's not one of those girls who look like they never eat, which I've never gone for anyway. She's tiny, though. I'm more than a head taller than she is.

If things were different, if I thought she was the kind of girl who was just looking for a good time, I'd see if she wanted to hook up. Doesn't take a genius to see that wouldn't be her, though.

"I just wanted to bring your sweatshirt back. I have this speech I have to write for FBLA. It's due in a few weeks and I need to work on it." Virginia takes a small step backward.

"FB what what?" I shake my head. It's Friday night. It doesn't matter what she has a speech for. Why would she be working on it tonight?

"Future Business Leaders of America. I should go..."

I step backward, too. I am definitely not a future business leader, unless you count Dad's shit as a business. Something tells me she wouldn't, and thinking about hooking up with this girl is a really stupid thing for me to do. "Yeah, you probably should."

"Ry! Come here for a second." At the sound of Luke's voice, I whip my head toward the porch.

"Hold up." I should have just told her bye. We both know she should leave, but she nods and I run over to my brother. "What's up?"

"Who is that?"

"Some girl I met. She's a little young for ya, don't you think?" Though if they were closer in age, I could see Luke with someone like her. He's a future business leader of America.

"Funny." He groans. "Listen, be careful. I don't know who she is, but she doesn't look like the kind of girl you'd usually hang out with. I don't want you—"

"Fuck you, Luke." Dude, I can't believe a few minutes ago I'd considered apologizing to him. He takes one look at Virginia and decides she's too good for me.

Not that I don't agree with him.

And not that I want her, either, but still.

"Ry, that's not—" He grabs my arm but I jerk it away, and then toss the twenty back at him.

"Whatever."

Nothing is going through my head as I take the stairs down. I have no plan, but still, when I get back to Virginia, I step close. Closer than I have been yet. Glancing over her shoulder, I catch Luke's eyes before paying attention to her again. I swear she smells like the ocean... like freedom.

Putting my hand flat on the car, I lean in. "Go to a party with me tonight."

"I don't go to parties," she stutters.

"Go with me anyway." Ocean hits me again.

She sighs and I know I have her. I don't move back as I wait for the yes, hoping to feel her breath on my neck, but it's Virginia who pulls away from me. I don't feel her breath, her answer vibrating through me instead.

"No."

Chapter Seven

Virginia

"You really like saying that word to me." Pierced-lip boy cocks his head slightly. "Come on. It'll be fun."

There are certain rules I've given myself. Ever since I can remember, rules have been important to me. They're important to Dad. Even though there were times Mom's lack of rules were fun, most of the time they just made me flustered, frantic, as though the control I hold so tightly in my fingertips is getting pried away.

Dad used to say that Mom's carefree ways were what first drew him to her. That was before any of the *other* Charitys showed up, when her lack of control had been more about fun. Or at least that's what everyone thought. Who really knows?

When I first started to discover what was going on around me, when I first decided what I wanted for my life, I put my rules into place. I knew that was the only way not to let Mom's curse claim me.

I do homework when it's assigned because there's no point in waiting. You never know when something will come up, and as dorky as it sounds, I really would much rather be safe than sorry.

I keep myself busy with school activities, because the more responsibility I have, the less space there is for distraction.

I always have a plan.

I avoid things that are creative, because artists and writers are flighty. They're selfish. Grandma was. In many ways, Mom is too.

I don't let boys distract me. They make you forget about your plan, and for me, that isn't an option.

Pierced-lip boy's eyes dart to the side slightly. I look over to see him watching the other guy as he walks to his car. Their eyes don't leave each other as he gets in, pulls forward, and then stops.

"We're a little busy here," he says, and for a second, I wonder about his name. He was called Ry…and I don't need to know more than that. It's not like I'll see him again.

"Remember what I said. I'm serious, bro."

The second he pulls away, pierced-lip boy steps backward. Wait. "Why'd you pull away?"

He cocks a brow. "You want me close?"

A stupid rush of heat pools in my belly. No, no, no. "Yeah right. It's just, you didn't get closer until he came out, and then the second he left…" *Oh.* "You were only acting like that to get under his skin! Why?" I'm surprised I said it, and annoyed I know it's true. On reflex, my hand shoots out and I smack his arm.

"Hey!" Pierced-lip boy holds up his hands. "No kicking my ass. Damn, you're feisty. I didn't ask you to go because of my brother, I asked you because you're hot."

My eyes stretch wide at that no matter how hard I try to fight it. It's not that I think I'm ugly, I don't. But I've also never had a boy come right out and tell me I'm hot. It's not logical, but I almost think boys at my school don't talk like that. In reality, they don't talk to *me* that way because they see me as too serious for it.

When I realize my lips are pulling into a smile, I bite down on my cheeks. He must notice, because he gets this look on his face. I've seen it in movies a million times—the cocky half grin, the intense eyes that feel like fingers brushing across your skin. Whoa, holy crap. Staring at his eyes for the first time in daylight, I can see they're totally different colors. One is blue, and the other is half-blue and half-brown. My resistance starts to weaken. His eyes look deep, as though there are more layers than he's showing.

"Go to the party with me, Virginia."

It's the name that pulls me out of his spell. Every time he says my name, he uses Virginia, even though I told him I go by Lulu. "No, thanks. I have a plan, and getting drunk at some stupid party isn't part of it."

I need to go before he weakens my defenses even more. He jerks back when I sit down and pull the door closed. Once it shuts, I turn on the ignition, ready to leave.

"Fine. Whatever. Have a good life, future business leader of America."

My hands fall away from the steering wheel, and before I know what I'm doing, I rip a piece of paper from the notebook on my passenger seat and write my phone number down.

He pauses when I hold the paper out. Looks down at it and then back at me. "I don't need this. I'm not trying to be a dick, but I'm not really the kind of guy who's going to call and spend hours talking to you on the phone every night. I'm not going to be your boyfriend. Find someone else for that."

Ugh. Of course he would think that's why I'm giving it to him. Actually, my only thought was that refusing to go to a party with some guy, only to hear about him killing himself driving drunk or *worse*, isn't in my plan.

I shove it into his hand. "And I'm not the kind of girl who sits around waiting to talk to a guy on the phone all night, either. I have much more important things going on than that. You're going to a party. I'm assuming you'll be drunk. If you need…well, you saved my life once, so I guess I owe it to you to return the favor. If you need a ride, call. Please. If not, feel free to lose it."

This time I don't hold myself back from driving away. When I get to the end of his driveway, my eyes dance toward the rearview mirror. He's standing where I left him, watching my car as I go.

Shaking all thoughts of boys with intense, multi-colored eyes, bad attitudes and pierced lips from my brain, I drive home.

Three hours later, I sit in the middle of my bed, with an open document in front of me. I haven't written a word of my speech. I tried going over the agenda for the next student council meeting as well, but the words go in, tumble around and then escape before I can process them.

I wonder what the guy in the car was so serious about—his brother? Definitely because they looked the same, minus the piercings. Same attitude. Same hair color. Same build.

I wonder why pierced-lip boy went rigid when his brother spoke.

I wonder why I can't stop thinking about him.

Just stop, I tell myself. I am in control of what I feel. I always will be. Refusing to sit here doing nothing a second longer, my fingers move across the keyboard and I make myself get to work.

Chapter Eight

Ryder

We're partying at Tanner's house tonight. He's the only one of us with money. His house is probably bigger than mine, Drea, Shane and Cody's combined. The only reason Tanner even goes to school with us is because he got kicked out of his private school.

His parents decided they didn't want him to embarrass them around their country club friends anymore, so they sent him to school in the ghetto. Tanner's parents are out of town. It wouldn't surprise me if they have the cops do drive-bys while they're gone, but Tanner doesn't seem to give a fuck, so I don't either.

"You're up, Ryder." Shane leans back in his chair as I sit forward. After drawing a card, I put my winning hand on the table and grin.

"Shit. I'm not playing this with you anymore. You always kick everyone's ass." Shane groans and pushes to his feet. "Let's go out back."

The other people at the table, most of whom we don't know,

stay there. Shane and I make our way to the backyard. People are everywhere, most of them congregating by the two kegs on either end of the lawn.

Shane walks around to the side of the house and unlatches the gate. Most people wouldn't know to come back here, except our friends. There's a small table with two chairs. Shane takes one of them, but I lean against the side of the house.

He pulls his pipe out of his pocket, packs it, and takes a hit. "How's shit with Luke? He still being a dick?"

Yeah. Just what I want to talk about tonight. "Always." After taking the pipe from him, I put it to my lips and inhale.

"Sucks."

"What about you?"

"I think my mom's usin' again. Can't tell for sure, though."

Shit. It makes me realize things with Luke could be a whole lot worse. Pot's one thing, but when his mom is using, she doesn't screw around. She does shit that's almost gotten her killed.

I lean my head back and look up, thinking it's definitely a good idea Virginia didn't come with me tonight. Shane wouldn't have talked about his mom around her, and he shouldn't have to worry about what he says. Who the hell knows what she would do if she heard something like that? I'm sure stressing about druggie parents isn't a part of her world. Or watching people get high.

A slow ache starts in my gut and moves up toward my chest. I'm suddenly pissed that she lives this perfect existence where she doesn't worry about stuff like this. Where she's so damn good that she has a *plan,* and she's too perfect to party. Where she'll get to grow up and be the next fucking future business leader of America and others like Shane and me won't have a chance.

"Let me know if you need anything. You know Luke won't care if you chill with us." My brother gives me shit about my friends, but he's pretty cool about helping if someone needs it. Shane has stayed with us off and on. We all know his mom isn't going to report him missing if he doesn't come home. It probably makes it easier on her when he's gone.

"Thanks, man." He holds out his hand and we bump fists.

"Thanks for ditching us in there! We went out to see if you guys left without telling us, but Shane's car is still here." Drea playfully elbows me in the stomach. "Assholes."

"You were with Tanner," I throw back at her. "It's his house. We figured you'd be okay with him and Cody."

Cody takes the seat across from Shane, pushing his dyed blond hair from his eyes. Tanner sits on his lap and says, "There's a bunch of idiots in there. Even I don't want to be around them."

"Want me to kick them out for you, baby?" Cody nuzzles Tanner's neck.

"Nope. Maybe they'll break something and I'll piss off my parents."

Cody laughs and kisses Tanner's neck again. He smiles when Tanner whispers something in his ear.

It's so strange watching the two of them together. Not because they're both guys, none of us give a shit about that, but because they obviously love each other and don't mind showing it. Cody was at our school before Tanner, but he never really hung out with us. When Tanner came, he sort of just fit right in with us from his first day. He wasn't there a month before he brought Cody out with us one night.

He said if we had a problem with it, we better say so. He was obviously testing us, but like I said, we've never given a shit who he was into. Cody became part of our group from that day on. If I'm being honest, we don't really know a lot about Cody other than the fact that he's Tanner's. It's been almost four years and they're still together.

None of us have parents who stay together like that. Well, except for Tanner, but they think they're better than us so they don't count. Drea's parents are off one week, on the next. It's really her stepdad, but he's been around forever. He comes and goes whenever the hell he wants, though. Shane doesn't know who his dad is, and my mom hasn't been around since I was a kid.

Luke never brings girls home. He's like Virginia; he has a *plan*, and girls aren't a part of it.

Tanner and Cody are the only happy couple I've ever known.

A floodlight on the side of the house shines down on us. Drea looks around. "Nice. You guys are gentlemen. No one is going to give me a seat?"

Tanner and Cody start whistling, and looking anywhere except at Drea. Shane taps his lap. "Sit down."

"Ha, ha." Drea rolls her eyes and punches his arm. Shane frowns, and then rubs it as she leans against the house next to me. The way she hit him makes me think about Virginia and the little slap she gave me on my arm earlier. Drea doesn't slap, she punches. Another difference between the rich girl and us.

She did give me her number, though. She doesn't know me. She definitely doesn't seem like the kind of girl who gives her phone number to just anyone. Why would she be so worried about a guy like me getting home safe? I've never needed anyone to worry about me before, not that I do now, but I have to admit it was pretty cool of her.

You saved my life once so I guess I owe it to you to return the favor.

Oh yeah, that's what it is. She thinks she owes me. I get that. Debts can bury you, no matter what kind they are. It's not that she gives a shit about me; she thinks she owes me.

"Ry, you want a hit?" Drea asks, and I realize Shane pulled out his pipe again.

"Nah, I'm cool." Pushing my hands into my pockets, I look up at the dark sky again.

If you need a ride, call. Please.

What the hell had the "please" been about? If it's because she owes me, why would it be so important that I call? That's what I don't get. My friends kick ass. I'm glad to have them, and I know they'd do anything for me, but they've never told me to call them if I'll be drinking at a party they're not at.

They finish smoking and then start talking about school and Tanner's parents. I'm half listening, half not. Then I'm trying to figure out why I'm not listening to them more instead of trying to dissect my conversation with the rich girl that I'll never see again.

The girl with the plan, who walked out onto a collapsing dock late at night... No matter how I look at it, nothing fits when it comes to her.

A warm body pulls up against my side. "Wanna fool around?" Drea asks.

I shake my head before I realize what I'm doing. There are zero reasons for me not to want to screw around with Drea. Unattached sex with a girl who wants nothing more than sex and friendship from me? I've always signed my name on that dotted line.

"Oh." Drea puts space between us.

My eyes shoot to Shane, who's looking at me like I just broke her heart and he's her protective Dad with a shotgun behind his back.

"I'm not really feelin' so hot," I say, lamely.

"He's just not man enough to handle you." Shane winks at her. This is what we do. We always have Drea's back.

Drea looks a little unsure of herself for a second, but then recovers quickly. "Eh, been thinking about trading him in for another plaything anyway. Thanks, Shane."

He gives her a simple nod. I nudge Drea's side, and she looks at me and smiles. A breath I didn't realize I held pushes from my lungs. I need to know we're okay. I wrap an arm around her shoulders and kiss her forehead. "You know I love you, Dre."

Until Dad comes back, these guys are the only people in my life who I know will always be there. No matter what Luke says, I know the second he's free of me, he'll be gone.

Chapter Nine

Virginia

There was once a girl named Control. There was nothing she needed more than her name. It was everything to her. It defined her.

~*~

My dad's a lawyer. When he and Mom were together, he rarely went out of town on business. He tried to stay home as much as possible. Now that I'm older, he leaves from time to time for a conference or something like that. It's not like he worries that he can't trust me.

I remember one time, he had a conference he couldn't get out of. He sat Mom and I down at the dining room table to talk about it. That's what Dad does—he talks. Mom creates when she's having a hard time—books or art, it doesn't matter. Dad talks. I look for distractions.

So, Dad sat us down to talk. It really wasn't a big deal, he said. It wasn't as if he didn't trust Mom with me. It wasn't as though she hadn't been doing well for a while, but we all knew there was a little worry when it came to him being gone for more than a workday.

One of her personalities, Samantha, had once thrown a party when Dad was at work. Not the kind of party most parents go to, either. Once Robin had been afraid someone would break in, and I had to hide with her in the closet until Dad got home.

Yes, I'm being serious. I can't put into words what it's like to see my own mom that way. To see her face, and her hair, and her hands. To recognize the scent of her, but to know she's not the one in control. That later she'll be back, and when she finds out what she's done, she'll be broken. That's typically when the depression would sink in.

Dad promised it would be okay. Mom promised she would be fine.

I knew otherwise.

Monday, things had been fine. Tuesday as well. Wednesday, I got up for school to see Mom sitting in a chair in my room watching me, practically bouncing with too much excitement.

"Finally! It's about time you got up. Let's go! I want to get out of here, and your dad will freak if I don't take you with me."

It wasn't Mom. It was Samantha.

"Where do you want to go?" I remember noticing the shake in my own voice.

"There's a concert in Los Angeles. If we leave soon, we can make it." She pushed to her feet.

My eyes darted to the side to look for the phone but it wasn't there.

"I took it. Like I didn't know the first thing you would do is try to call your dad. He ruins all the fun."

My heart beat so hard it started to hurt. "I can't go. I have school. They'll call Dad if I'm not there."

"And we'll already be on the road by then. If I leave you here, you'll call him the second I go. Come on. What kind of kid are you? You're supposed to want adventure. You're supposed to want excitement!"

That had been the first time I wondered if something was wrong with me. If I had it wrong and she was right. If being responsible didn't mean I *was* crazy. What kind of kid told on their own parent?

A little burst of excitement lit under my skin. It felt like a mini-explosion. I'd never been to L.A. It could be fun taking the six-hour drive.

"Seriously, show me you're not such a bore. Let's go, Lulu." Calling me a bore was the reminder that feeling excitement over something like this was wrong. I didn't want to be like her. She was Samantha and she did crazy things and caused problems for Dad and I.

Even when she was Mom, she was the girl whose mother had left her when she was a teen. She'd never told anyone, deciding to be homeless instead, painting murals around the cities she visited and writing stories about them.

She'd told me most of the stories.

Right then, she was Samantha, and Samantha hated me because I was a responsibility.

"I won't tell. I promise. Just go." It wasn't like I couldn't get myself to school okay for a few days. Even then I'd known it.

"Don't have to tell me twice." She'd made her way to the door and stopped. "Are you sure, kid? It'll be a blast. Live a little."

I'd paused. Really paused. Then I shook my head and she left.

It was the first time I hated my mom, because for a second,

she'd made me want to go. That scared me more than anything. I'd almost lost control and done something reckless. I'd wanted to.

I don't know why, but it's that story that plays in my head as Hailey and Jamie try and talk to me over lunch. No, not just talk, we do that every day. I knew that sooner or later they would ask me about the incident at school. I guess they'd been biding their time, waiting to ambush me.

There's brief seconds where I want to tell them everything, and that scares the crap out of me.

"Ah." I nod my head. That's where the memory came from, because I almost let go of my control today, just like I had that day.

"Ah, what?" Jamie asks, a heavy weight in her eyes. She cares. They both do. I get that. But how can I tell Mom's secret? She's been able to keep it all this time. We've been able to keep it. I'd be lying if I pretended that someone finding out didn't scare the crap out of me.

It would make my life-story true.

It would take the control that I so need out of my hands.

"Nothing." I shake my head. "The *ah* meant nothing, and the thing the other day wasn't that big a deal. It's not even worth talking about. Did you guys start your essay?"

"Lulu, that wasn't nothing the other day. That was—"

"Please," I cut Hailey off. "Please. I can't... I just can't." It isn't much, but it's all I can give them. I don't want to keep secrets from my friends. Again, I wish I could open my mouth and let it all spill out, but what if they look at me differently? It's one of my biggest fears—for the people I care about to look at me and wonder if I'm crazy. To wonder if I could grow up and be like Mom, who isn't always Mom at all.

I don't want to be different.

It's Jamie who speaks first. She starts talking about her essay. From the looks they share with each other, it's obvious that I let them down, but I grab onto the subject change like a lifeboat.

The rest of the day goes smoothly. Hailey, Jamie and I laugh and talk during our free time in FBLA.

I feel at my most normal when I'm with my friends. I know I'm lucky to have them, and again, I think about telling them, but the words are still stuck in my throat like they've always been. I don't even like to talk to Dad about it, because I've seen the look in his eyes, too. I've seen him wonder if I will somehow end up with the same curse the other women in my family have.

I'm on my way to my locker when Mrs. Young, the English teacher, stops me. "Lulu, have you put anymore thought into that writing competition I want you to enter? I know you're all set up for college, but this will look good. There's no one here who has the chance to win it, except you."

No, no I haven't thought about it. I'd tried to forget about it if I'm being honest. I don't care if it's a major award or how good it will look for college. I don't care about an extra scholarship. I don't want that creative part of me to exist.

"Thanks, but I can't. I already have so much going on with school, FBLA, and student council." As I speak, I'm walking backward away from her. My ribs are shrinking into my chest.

Mrs. Young's face falls. "Lulu."

"Thanks for thinking of me!" And then I run out. There are zero parts of me who want to do this, and I won't. I don't care what anyone says. I don't care how good I am or who gets upset about it. I don't write. Not if I don't have to.

Dad's working late tonight, so I start dinner on my own. The spaghetti is almost done when I hear the front door open and close. A few seconds later, Dad walks into the kitchen.

"Smells good," he tells me.

"Thanks!"

We sit down to eat, and he tells me about his day and asks about mine. I love these times with him. It reminds me of families on TV shows, those people whose lives seem too perfect. Even when they don't, everything is wrapped up in thirty minutes or less.

"Hey, Lu?" he says when we're cleaning up.

"Yeah?"

"Your mom says you haven't answered her phone calls, and that you haven't returned any of them."

My stomach drops out. First the conversation with Hailey and Jamie, then Mrs. Young and the writing, and now this. "I don't know how to talk to her, Dad. Please don't push me. I…." I don't have to finish before his eyes grow sad. Just like I did with Jamie and Hailey, I know I've disappointed him.

Chapter Ten

Ryder

On my tenth birthday Dad took me out on a job for the first time. All I did was stand on the corner as a lookout. Even though my hands shook the entire time, I felt like 'The Fucking Man'— like I was important; like they couldn't pull the job without me. I was the guy who made sure nothing went down.

Even though it wasn't a planned gig, they knew what they were doing. It didn't take Dad long to get into the store—it never did. In and out, that's what Dad always said. In and out in under ninety seconds. It was thirty seconds when some guy tried to turn down the alley. I had less than a minute to get him as far away as I could, or he'd see them coming out with things they shouldn't have.

And I'd done it. Dad and his friends gave me a small cut and a beer that night. They called me a man. They said I'd saved the day. I'd never really saved anything before, but the words were like a fucking rush. Even then I knew I wanted to hold onto that feeling.

After that, Dad decided birthdays were lucky. His birthday,

mine, Luke's. We always did something big after that; usually something illegal, but we were always lucky and we always celebrated big.

That's why I find someone to buy me a twelve-pack of beer tonight, and that's why I buy a bunch of food that costs more than the shit we normally buy, wishing for the millionth time that I could just take it. It's Dad's birthday, and Luke and I should celebrate it the way Dad would do for us.

Luke sighs as he closes the door. He's wearing his standard uniform, black pants and a Polo shirt. He got his hair trimmed so it's shorter than mine, clean cut. He turns and sees me sitting on the couch with a beer in my hand. His eyes dart toward the kitchen, and there's all sorts of crap in there. Way too much food for the two of us.

"What the hell are you doing, Ry? And who said you can drink?"

I don't know why, but I let him rip the can from my hand.

"Where'd you get the money for this?" Luke runs a hand through his hair. "Jesus, don't tell me you're stealing or selling drugs. Third strike. Why do I have to keep reminding you of this?"

Anger erupts inside me, a seething volcano that has no choice but to release its wrath. My legs shake as I shove to my feet, ignoring that twitch in the side of my head. "Like I could ever forget if I wanted to. All you do is shove it down my throat! I don't know what the fuck I was thinking trying to be cool with you. It's not like you ever wanted to be a part of this family."

I try to head for the door but Luke grabs my arm. "Are you kidding me? I'm here, aren't I? He's the one who's not. He's the one who chose dirty jobs over us and then bailed. Where'd the money come from man?" he asks again.

I sold my hoodie to a kid at school who wanted it. Tanner gave me some shit out of his house that his parents would never know was gone, so I sold those too. I might as well have stolen it, the way Luke's acting. At least I'd be getting in trouble for actually doing the one thing I'm good at.

Luke's fingers dig into my arm, his eyes holding mine, both of them fiery.

"Stealing," I lie. "What else? You're lucky it's something small and not B&E or jacking a car. I'm good at that shit."

It's then that Luke's eyes soften. My body gets tighter, more wound-up, a shaken can ready to explode.

"Celebrating his birthday isn't going to make him come back for you."

Boom.

The lid bursts off and I jerk my arm free of Luke's hold. "Maybe it's because of you. He won't come back for me because you're here and he knows you'd rat him out."

I make it to the door before Luke says, "Don't go, Ry. Why are we always doing this? You're my brother. Talk to me."

Wrong. He hates Dad, and I know that's who he sees when he looks at me. Everyone says I'm just like Dad. I'm the guy who Luke assumes is selling drugs, stealing, or the one he thinks will hurt Virginia. "*You're* always doing this, not me. And we're not brothers in the ways that matter."

You can't choose your blood. You don't have to want to be with them. Luke has no choice but to be here with me, even though it's not what he wants. I'd choose water over blood any day. I slam the door behind me.

Tanner had my back today. Shane, Dre and Cody would, too, and not because they have to but because they want to.

I have no choice but to walk. I could call Shane, but I don't feel like partying tonight. He'd be cool and chill with me, but why should I screw up his fun just because my brother is an asshole?

My dad once told me that he liked having a place outside of town because there weren't as many eyes on him. It made sense to me, and it never really bothered me until tonight, but it's dark as hell out here. Quiet. I'm not real used to quiet.

And it's a long ass walk for me to get anywhere.

When the wind blows, I shove my hands in my pocket, hoping it will help to keep them warm. My body shivers but I ignore it and keep going.

It was so fucking stupid to sell my hoodie to try and have a cool night with my brother. It would have been easy for me to get what I wanted without it costing a dime.

Like Dad said, I'm a ghost. It's easy for me to grab what I need. It's why they started taking me with them. I remember each and every job, remember when they told me how good I was and how good I would be. They used to tell Dad how lucky he was to have me for a son.

Luke might be perfect in his world, but he doesn't have the respect I do in mine.

I walk for an hour before a light mist of rain starts hitting my skin. My fingers hold onto my phone. I should call Shane, or Drea. Her house isn't far from here, and even if we have to go chill in the shed out back, it'd be dry. It's where she goes when she needs to be alone.

For some reason, though, I keep going.

If you need a ride, call. Please.

Virginia...I could call her. She owes me.

A door slams in my brain, closing those thoughts down before they can grow wings and take flight. The rich girl has better things to do than coming out here to pick up my ass, even if it's homework or whatever she thinks is so important.

Plus, I've always been able to take care of myself, so when a car comes by, I stick my arm out with my thumb up.

Of course, the car passes. Then another. It's the third car that pulls over. My eyes get big when I see it's a woman old enough to be my grandma.

"You getting in or what, kid?" she asks.

"Are you sure?" sort of tumbles out of my mouth. Grandmas don't usually pick up kids who look like me.

"If you're stupid enough to question a ride in the cold, maybe I'm not."

An unexpected chuckle falls out of my mouth and I get in. She turns up the heat and I rub my arms to warm up.

"Where you going?" Grandma asks.

"Um…anywhere. Can you drop me off in town?"

"You okay?"

"Yeah."

She turns up the country music as though the conversation is over. Fine with me. We drive for about ten minutes or so when we come up on the stretch of ocean I came to with my friends the other night. It's kind of like a ghetto beach where no one goes because they know kids like me hang out there.

The light rain has already stopped. It's like that here. One second it's dry and the next a fucking storm is slamming down on you.

I lean forward when I notice a car parked ahead. It looks like whoever owns it tried to hide it in a dark corner of the beach parking.

When Grandma's lights hit it, I recognize the vehicle.

Virginia.

Before I can slam the door on the words, like I did on my thoughts earlier, my mouth opens and they come rushing out. "Stop. You can let me out here."

Chapter Eleven

Virginia

Dad trusts me. He always has. I've never given him a reason not to. I've never gotten into trouble or lied. I've never been late coming home or had a problem telling him where I am. Because of that, I don't have a curfew. I tell Dad where I'm going and what I'm doing and when I'll be home. As long as it's reasonable, he's okay with it.

Tonight is the first time in my life I've ever lied to my dad about what I'm doing. I don't even know why I did it. The need to be alone became a magnet. The beach, *this* stretch of beach is the other half, pulling me in. Dad understands wanting to be alone. He wouldn't understand sitting on an empty beach in a town that's not known for its upstanding citizens.

Even I don't understand it.

So I'd lied. I'm supposed to be having a movie marathon with Hailey. I'll text to let him know if I'm coming home or staying over. I'm officially a liar. That's not someone I ever thought I'd be and I hate it.

"It's a little cold for almost drowning tonight," says a deep voice from behind me. "I don't have to worry about you going back onto the deathtrap, do I?"

I whip my head around. A heavy, shaky breath deflates my lungs. It's pierced-lip boy. I knew that before I turned, but it still makes my body relax to see him with my own eyes.

"Oh look, you brought a lantern. How Virginia of you."

He's not wearing a jacket, which surprises me. I have my coat on and a blanket wrapped around me and I'm still not exactly warm. "You don't know enough about me to say what's 'Virginia' of me or not." Did that come out right? This whole conversation feels weird considering I'm talking about myself.

He doesn't move, just stands next to me, looking down. There's a shadow in his eyes I didn't notice the other two times I've seen him, or maybe it wasn't there. His body language is different too, heavier, if that makes sense.

He shrugs. "I don't have to know you well to see that's something you would do, and I never would. That most of my friends never would, either. I know you're a planner. You must have known you were coming out here tonight instead of it happening by accident, like it did the first time."

A gasp comes out of my mouth. I didn't tell him that I hadn't planned to be here the first night, yet he knows. And I definitely wasn't coming without some sort of light when I knew I'd be here tonight.

"Bet you even have a weapon." He cocks a brow, but there's something forced about it.

"Shut up." I turn away from him. "Or I'll use it on you." Yes, there's a bat under the blanket next to me. There's nothing wrong with being a smart girl, even when I am moping on a beach at night.

His voice sounds far off when he replies, "You're smart. That's a good thing."

When I look up again, he's staring out at the water. He's shivering, but it looks like he's trying to hide it. I have no business being out here with this boy. No business being out here at all, but especially with him. Still, watching him stand next to me as he looks at the black water in front of us, I wonder if he can somehow feel like I do. Trapped. Scared. Cursed. Alone.

"Obviously smarter than you. It was sprinkling a little while ago. I can't believe you came out without your jacket. Sit down. You can use some of my blanket. I don't want you to get pneumonia or something."

Pierced-lip boy glances down. He gives me a half-grin, looking more like the guy I've seen before, while at the same time as though he's slipping on a mask. "It's okay to want to be close to me, Virginia."

No, this boy is nothing like me. I don't even know how I thought that. "Ugh. Could you be more arrogant? You're not my type at all."

My heart does this funny, rapid beat, slow down thing when he sits beside me. I pause a minute, trying to will my arm to stop shaking as I untangle it from the blanket and offer him part of it.

"Nah, I'm good."

Pause.

"So, what is?" he stays looking at me. He doesn't skirt away from eye contact, I've noticed. Lots of the people I know do.

"What is what?"

"Your type. Tell me what rich girl Virginia—the girl with a plan, who likes to hang out at ghetto beach with a lantern and a weapon, but who also does her homework on weekends—looks for in a guy. I'm sure you have a list."

"Why? Because I'm a girl, right? We all have to dream about

having the perfect boyfriend? Someone who will, what…save us? Protect us?" My arm shoots out and I elbow him. This time, my heart freezes. I don't even know this boy, yet I just elbowed him. And he *is* the kind of boy who belongs on what he calls "ghetto beach," when we both know I don't.

My body relaxes when he laughs. "I have a feeling that the night I helped you on the dock is probably the first time someone has had to save you, Virginia Woolf. It will probably be the last, too."

"Don't." I shake my head. Heat, such a contrast to the weather, burns through me. "Don't call me Virginia Woolf."

He cocks his head, as though I'm a Rubik's cube he's trying to solve. "Sorry. You said your mom named you after her. Didn't realize it was a biggie. Who is Virginia Woolf, anyway?"

At this, I can't stop my eyes from growing wide. "Are you kidding me?" Yeah, he probably isn't as homework-oriented as I am, but how does someone not know who Virginia Woolf is? Do they teach at his school? "She was a writer."

"I'm kidding, rich girl. I'm not that dumb. Your mom a writer or something? She must at least be super fucking into books if she named you after her."

My arms tighten around my knees, frustration making my muscles tight. "Yes." Most people know who Charity Nichols is. She's famous. She's talented. She's inspiring. No one knows she's been more than one person.

"I bet you are, too, huh? Shit like that normally runs in families."

It's as though his words turn my insides into cement. My whole body goes rigid. "No. I hate writing. I don't do it unless I have to." I won't become cursed. I won't lose myself so deeply in fiction that I can't handle the real world.

And then, because I want to get the conversation off me, I ask, "What about you? What did you inherit from your parents?"

This time, it's him who goes stiff. "My mom bailed when I was young. I don't know much about her."

My heart does this softening thing.

He says, "Don't feel bad for me. Fuck her. If she didn't want me, then I don't want her. My dad is cool, though."

"Okay, then what did you inherit from him? My dad and I both like rules. He likes numbers, and I do as well."

Pierced-lip boy shakes his head, chuckling softly. I feel my cheeks start to redden. "What? There's nothing wrong with liking numbers and rules."

"Hey." He holds his hands up as though he's trying to show he doesn't mean to attack me. "I'm not saying there is. I'm just thinking you probably don't want to know what I learned from my pops. We'll leave it at that."

Again, I notice his hands shake from the cold. I think he sees me watching and he jerks his arms down. Rolling his eyes, he grins as though he thinks I'm being ridiculous.

"Your eyes are two different colors." I don't know why I just brought that up to him. Duh. Like he doesn't know what colors his eyes are. Not once in my life have I talked to a boy about his eyes.

"Hot, isn't it?" His smile grows, and I feel the urge to hit him with my bat.

"Yeah, but it quickly gets canceled out by your mouth." My mouth drops open when I realize what I said. Yes, he is cute. I've never liked a boy with facial piercings, and honestly never thought I would, but they suit him. He has a nice smile, when he's not being a jerk. The tousled hair thing usually isn't for me, but on him it is. "Not that…you aren't…I didn't mean."

For what feels like the millionth time he shakes his head, as though I'm being ridiculous. "It's okay to admit when you think someone is good-looking. I don't know why people are so weird about sex. Especially girls. It's annoying that people freak out when a girl admits she's into sex. There's nothing wrong with wanting it, or admitting to it."

Wait. "What? I never said I was into sex. Not that I'm *not* into sex… I mean…ugh! Stop laughing at me!" I bury my face in my hands. Why the heck does he get me so tongue-tied?

When he finally stops laughing, I see his teeth chatter. He's cold. And he should be. "Shut up," I say again, and then I unwrap the blanket from around my right side, still keeping it around my left shoulder, and stretch it out to him. He pauses a second, watching me—no, *dissecting* me—like he's trying to see everything inside me to figure out how I work. Then he takes it, scoots closer to me and wraps the blanket around his shoulders as well.

We're both quiet for a minute before he says, "Don't worry about it. I think you're beautiful, too."

Wow. Not hot. *Beautiful.* A shiver runs through me, even though I suddenly feel warm. He called me hot before, but hot and beautiful are two different things. When he moves even closer to me, I let him.

He isn't part of my plan, and I'm not good at change. I've always needed to be the one who decides what will happen to me, instead of letting things happen on their own. This guy came out of nowhere, and though my instinct is to walk away, I don't. I don't even know if I'll see him again after tonight. There's a quiet whisper, deep in the darkest parts of me. I don't know if it was there before and I ignored it, but that voice wants to enjoy this night. I can go back to my plan tomorrow.

Chapter Twelve

Ryder

If I were here with Drea, it would just be normal to share a blanket with her. I wouldn't give a shit if she knew I was freezing my balls off. Hell, I'd even wrap myself in a blanket with Tanner and Cody if I needed to keep warm. Cold is cold, and they're my friends. But when Virginia asked me the first time, the shock got pushed away by pride. I didn't want her to know I was so cold I felt numb. I could handle it.

When she held the blanket out to me a second time, there's no way I could say no. I can't even say it's because of the temperature, either. This girl doesn't go around sharing a blanket with guys on the beach. She definitely doesn't do it with guys like me. I got the same feeling in my chest that I did when she gave me her number. I don't get why a girl like her would care if I'm cold, or if I have wheels when I need them, but she does, and it makes this strange sort of happiness go off inside me—little firecrackers I've never experienced.

It's that unbalanced feeling she gives me that makes me ask, "Why were you out on the dock that night? You don't do shit like that."

She takes a deep breath. I feel the fabric of her jacket against my arm. It's warm, but I would rather it be skin. I wasn't lying when I said she's beautiful. She *is*. And the more I'm around her, the more I start to want her.

"How do you know?"

I don't know... "Come on, Virginia. You're stalling. It's not like I'm going to tell anyone. Hell, it's not like you can't tell that everything about me is more fucked up than you doing a little exploring on a dock." A part of me wants that last sentence back. People knowing who and what I am has never bothered me before, but with her, I suddenly don't want to draw more attention to the fact that my life is screwed up. Because it is. Even though I'm cool with the life I've led, I know it's fucked up.

"What are you doing out here tonight?"

Ah, so she's going to respond to a question with one of her own. I don't really have anything to hide, though. Scratch that. I have shit she doesn't need to know, but this isn't one of them. "I got in a fight with my brother. He's an asshole."

"What about?" she asks.

There's a slight twitch in my chest at this question, but nothing too major. "I bought beer and a shit ton of food to celebrate my dad's birthday. He got pissed and then accused me of selling drugs or stealing everything."

She shivers, making me wonder if she's cold or if she's responding to what I said. Damn...maybe I went too far. I shouldn't have told her; but then, why does it matter? This is who I am. There's no changing me, and beautiful or not, I don't chill with people who give me hell for who I am.

"You brought *beer* into your house for your dad's birthday? And wait, why wouldn't your brother want to celebrate?"

I wait for the real question, because I know it's coming. This time, she doesn't surprise me.

"Did you? Steal? Or do you sell drugs?"

The fabric of her jacket doesn't touch my arm anymore. I'm caught between wanting the warmth back and being pissed at her questions. Of course she would assume, just like Luke did. It's the reaction I expect. She's a rich girl, and I'm trash. It is what it is.

"It's not the first time I've brought beer into my house, and it probably won't be the last. My dad doesn't live with us, and even if he did, he wouldn't care. He'd drink with me. Luke thinks he's too good for us, that's why he didn't want to celebrate."

I wait for her to pull the blanket away, too. Wait for her to get up. Wait for her to look at me like she doesn't know what she's doing here with me, because I don't know, either. Or why I'm here with her.

"I'm sorry... I didn't know. I shouldn't have asked like that."

Breath leaves my lungs when her fluffy coat touches my arm again. *What about the last question?* I want to ask her. Doesn't she want to know if she's sitting here with a thief or a druggie? Now my anger is aimed her way for a different reason. She should want to know that. She shouldn't just let that go. Not a girl like her.

"I don't sell drugs. I didn't steal the stuff. I sold my hoodie and some other things."

The light from the lantern flickers in her wide, green eyes. I smell her sweet scent mixed with ocean.

73

"That's why you don't have a jacket on tonight?"

"It's not a big deal. I'll get another one."

Now I'm waiting for something else—to see pity in her eyes. I hate that shit, and I might lose it if she feels bad for me. It doesn't come, though. There's something else in her eyes now—it almost looks like respect.

There have only been a few times in my life anyone looked at me like I'd done something important. When I'd jack something for Dad and his guys; when Shane and I beat a few guys' asses for giving Drea shit.

And now.

What I don't get is why selling my jacket would make her look at me like I'm something.

It's on the tip of my tongue to ask her, but I'm not sure I want the answer. There's shit I've done for Drea and Dad to be proud of me, but there's nothing I could have done to deserve this girl seeing me that way.

"I always play by the rules. Always." Her voice is soft. She's staring downward at the blanket around us instead of at me. I want her eyes my way, but I'm scared if I push it, she'll stop talking.

There's never been anything in my life that's scared me before.

"I need it," she continues. "I know it sounds ridiculous, and to most people it probably is, but I need stability. I need my plans, and to be in control. Other people do crazy and reckless things. I don't. I..."

When she doesn't keep going, I scoot closer to her. It's probably a stupid thing to do; this girl would be smart to get away from me. But she doesn't move, so I put my arm around her. My fingers crave skin again, but all I get is the jacket.

The firecrackers start going off for the second time, then slowly—so slowly I'm not even sure she's really doing it—Virginia lays her head on my shoulder.

I've held girls before—I've held Drea too many times to count—but it's never made my body feel like it's coming alive from the inside out.

"I had to deal with something I haven't had to see in a long time. It scared me. I knew it was reckless to go out on that dock. I knew it was stupid but still, something inside me wanted to go out there. I didn't want to get hurt, I just... I felt trapped, and somehow going out there made me feel free. I can't," she lifts her head. "I won't do something like that again. I got it out of my system, and that's the end of it."

So many things dance in her eyes, some out in the open, others hiding. Most of it is a mystery to me, but I know there is more to this girl than I thought. She's dealing with more than she shows the world.

And I suddenly want to be the one she lets inside to see it all. I want to be the one who makes her see it's okay to live.

"Nothin' wrong with losing control once in a while, Virginia."

Letting go of the blanket, I let my right hand touch her cheek, lift her chin so she's looking at me, and then keep letting it drift back until it makes a home against her neck.

Her skin feels as good as I thought it would—warm and soft. Reckless, in a way I've never experienced. "It can be fun." Lowering my mouth, I touch my lips to hers.

Chapter Thirteen

Virginia

As his mouth covers mine, fear pummels me, a wave going over my head like I'm trapped on a broken dock, scared that I might die. My reflex is to jerk back, to take a breath because air is something I need, and it's okay to need that.

My vision is lost to anything except blue and brown, the twist in his eyes, the questions there, the comfort. The last part isn't something I'd expect from a boy like him, and it makes another wave of fear threaten to drown me. But then his thumb brushes my neck and a tingle in my stomach makes my body shiver. It feels so good. *He* feels so good that I forget there's the worry of drowning.

I lean closer to him, and that's all the incentive he needs to take my mouth again. His tongue is at my lips, and I'm opening them to let him in. There's tasting and touching and a twisting together of tongues. I giggle into his mouth at how my thoughts are all coming out in "T" words, and he chuckles as though he hears them.

The laughing lends only a quick interruption, not that I want one, before he's kissing me again, and it's all I can feel or think about. It's all I want to know.

The studs of his piercings press into my skin, not painful, but reminding me they're there.

He tastes like the air after rain—clean...new and almost like being reborn.

His hand feels big on my neck, but he's gentle, much gentler than he seems when he tangles his fingers in my hair.

Just like everything is with him, the kiss is intense, urgent, fast moving. It was almost like he was born from the dark, coming out of nowhere the first night we met. Before I knew what was happening, he was there, his voice asking if I was hurt, his hand grabbing me to save me.

His lips are the same; they weren't there and then they were, and now he's wrapped around me, lowering me to the beach, a weight that freaks me out while grounding me at the same time.

My body pulses when his warm hand slides under my coat, under my shirt to touch the bare skin of my belly.

"Wait." The palm of my hand lands on his chest. "Not...not so fast."

And then his lips are gone. It's seriously like this guy is a magician or something, the way he's there and then he's not.

"Shit. Sorry. Wanted to feel your skin."

Holy wow. Those words echo through me, a pebble getting thrown into the water, little pulsing waves drifting from where it landed.

It's then I realize that I really am lying on my back, and he's lying on top of me. With one of his hands, he pushes the hair out of my face, and I want to ask him how it felt—my skin, that is. He wanted to touch it, and I want to know what it was like. Nothing comes out of my mouth, though. It doesn't surprise me when he speaks. He says whatever is on his mind all the time.

"This is so strange…" His voice has this far-off sound to it.

My body goes tense. "Great. Just what a girl wants to hear when a boy kisses her."

He smiles, and it makes me smile in return because for the first time, it's not a cocky grin.

"That's not what I meant. I just…you're like this compulsion I don't understand. It's like…" He shakes his head and then continues. "If I keep my hands to myself, can I kiss you again?"

I'm not sure what it says about me that he says I'm like a compulsion and then I want him to kiss me again. Maybe I'm more like Mom than I thought. My brain starts going haywire at the thought, memories and fears firing off in rapid succession.

Still, I nod my head and his mouth is moving with mine again, and it somehow quiets the noise inside my head.

Which is wrong. So, so wrong. But I always do what's right, and that hasn't helped Mom. It still hasn't stopped her from creating Amelia and threatening the world I've built for myself.

He drops his forehead to mine. "You're tense. If you don't want—"

"I want." There isn't time to be embarrassed by my declaration before he's kissing me again. More fresh-air taste. He lets his tongue retreat so mine can venture into his mouth.

I want, I want, I want, keeps going through my head and I can't help but try to remember the last time I really wanted something. Something that didn't revolve around Mom being okay, or keeping our secret, or doing everything in my power not to become a victim of our curse.

I want him. Not to have sex with him I mean, but I want *him.* I wanted to go to that party with him, and I wanted him to use my phone number, and I wanted to see him, which is why I brought him his hoodie. I wanted him to stay when he tried to walk away that first night, and I wanted to see him tonight. Why else did I come here?

There once was a girl named Want…

No, no, no. It's like he's taking my control, and part of me is glad. I don't even know him, but I still see that I've never known someone who is like him. There's something there, under the surface that he hides behind his attitude and I want to know what it is. I realize then that he's like a compulsion I don't understand, either.

And part of me likes it.

"Virginia." He kisses the corner of my mouth. "You." His lips find my neck next. "Stopped." They slide down and land on the hollow spot behind my ear. "Kissing."

A thought enters my head as if it suddenly planted there. "I don't even know your name." Oh God. I kissed a boy when I don't even know his name.

With that, he leans up slightly. There is still the feel of his body aligned with mine, but we're eye to eye now. "What?"

"Your name. I don't even know your name. You never told me. I'm assuming it's Ryan because your brother called you Ry, but, *oh my God,* you're lying on top of me right now and I don't even know your name!"

His breath brushes across my face when a laugh jumps from his mouth. It's like that first night when he laughed to break the uncomfortable silence.

Everything he does is contagious, and then I'm laughing, too. Our bodies are vibrating against each other as we both lose it over something that shouldn't be funny at all.

"What's wrong with me?" I finally gasp out. "I shouldn't

think this is funny. I don't know why I'm laughing."

Suddenly there is no earthquake inside our bodies as we're both still as he says, "Nothing."

"Nothing what?"

"Nothing is wrong with you. And Ryder. I'm Ryder, not Ryan."

Ryder. I like that. "I'm scared," I say, instead of…what? It's nice to meet you?

Ryder frowns. "Of me?"

Head shake.

Open mouth.

Words spill out. "No…of me." That's exactly how my actions feel, as though someone else is responsible for them and not me.

He twists a lock of my hair around his finger. "You're not scary. Except when you hit me. Then you're a little scary. I get being afraid of me, but not of yourself. You're…I don't know what you are, but there's nothing to be afraid of. I have a feeling you're the kind of girl who will always make sure she's okay."

Yes. That's who I want to be. "What are we doing?"

This time, Ryder pauses. He's usually so quick with his words. There's a shift and then he rolls off of me. My hand tightens in his shirt, and I realize for the first time that I'm holding onto him. Ryder doesn't go far, though, he just moves to his side, looking down at me. *Twist, twist, twist.* His finger still works my hair around itself. "I don't know," he finally admits.

I don't, either, but I want to keep doing it. And that might be the scariest admission of all.

Chapter Fourteen

Ryder

We were quiet in the car as she drove me home last night. I told her thanks and I'd call her. Ever since I left her, all I can think about is that I didn't kiss her goodnight and I didn't give her my phone number. What the fuck is wrong with me? Why wouldn't I kiss her goodbye? Why didn't I give her my number? And then the big question rains down on me—a barrage of punches like that fight Shane, me, Tanner and Cody got into with some punks at the mall this one time—why am I tripping out about her? She's not a big deal. She shouldn't matter.

But she does.

I'd been thinking about her so much. I couldn't sleep so I'd gotten out of bed and done my homework. I'm not like her. Most of the time, homework isn't even on my radar.

It's sixth period now, and my mind still isn't with me, which is crazy. I'm obsessing, when I've never obsessed about anything in my life.

"Okay, class, pass your homework assignments to the front of the room." Mr. Miller's monotone voice grabs my attention.

I grab my backpack off the floor and open it. Shane's sitting in front of me and he turns, probably because he hears me shuffle. One of his eyebrows shoots up when he sees me digging through my bag. "What? I did that shit last night. Did you?"

He nods, which doesn't really surprise me. People who don't know him don't expect it about him, but Shane's typically pretty good with school stuff.

I go back to looking through my bag, but it's not there. I double check, pretty annoyed because I finally took the time to do it, and what? I left it at home.

"Shit."

"Watch your language in my class, Mr. Blackstock. Is there a problem?"

Of course he would have to hear me. "I can't find my homework."

I watch as the bastard actually rolls his eyes. "Oh, so we're expected to believe you actually took the time to do your assignment for once, only you just so happened to lose it? Nice try, Mr. Blackstock. You don't do the work, you don't get any credit. You know how it goes by now."

One of my hands tightens into a fist and I get that twitch in my forehead. I don't give a shit if he gives me credit or lets me turn it in late, but he doesn't have to be a dickhead and accuse me of lying about it. I've had no problem admitting to not doing my work in the past, and today isn't any different. "I'm pretty sure I said I did it. I'm also pretty sure I didn't ask you to give me credit or to believe anything."

He eyes me with disgust. I can tell he's pissed I didn't keep my mouth shut and take his crap. Not my style.

"And now you can leave my classroom. Go to the principal's

office."

What. The. Fuck. "Why?" A few people snicker behind me, but I don't care who they are or what they think.

"For disrupting my class. Talking back. Not doing your homework *again*. You can take your pick."

"Are you shitting me?"

"Add cursing to your list of offenses, Mr. Blackstock. Now please go. I'd like to continue teaching the students who actually want to learn."

Motherfucker. This is the stuff Luke doesn't get. Dad was right. Most people don't give a shit about us. They'll find any excuse to look down on people like us...people they don't think are good enough for them. This is why I typically don't try. "Fine by me." I shove to my feet.

I make it halfway to the door when I hear, "Where do you think you're going, Mr. Mitchell?"

Fucking Shane.

"I didn't do it, either, so why wait for you to play your power trip and kick me out?"

"Both of you better make it to the principal's office, or it will be considered skipping."

The door slams behind us the second Shane and I make it into the hallway. I shove him. "What the fuck, man? You just said you did your homework. You should have stayed."

"Why? He was a dickhead to you. It's not like it matters, anyway. Come on, let's go before they send the rent-a-cop looking for us."

For a second I wonder if Virginia has security at her school. I bet she goes to a place where she doesn't have to worry about stuff like that. Then I think I'm fucking crazy for thinking about her. Again.

"Are you sure you don't wanna go back? I can chill and wait for you guys." Shane's smarter than me. He might not do a lot with it, but he has more to claim than being good at stealing like me. He's good at riding his board, too.

"Fuck you, man. Let's go across the street and wait for everyone to get out of school."

Our school is kind of in the middle of nowhere. We jog through the parking lot and across the street. There's a path through the woods where people go to skip or smoke.

It's quiet when Shane and I get there, as we both sit on one of the logs we use for chairs. My cell jabs into my hip so I pull it out of my pocket, rolling it around in my hand.

"I'll text Dre and tell her to let Tanner and Cody know where we are." Shane already has his phone in his hand. As he starts sending the message, my fingers move along the screen of my cell as well.

Hey

Virginia texts back almost immediately. **Who is this?**

Ryder. Forget my name already? You just learned it.

Funny. Why are you texting during school???

A laugh jumps out of my mouth. Who the hell is this girl? **Cuz I'm a rebel.**

"What are you laughing at?" Shane asks.

"Some chick." The words taste bitter on my tongue. Shane probably thinks she's some girl I'm fucking. "A friend, or something," I add, though that doesn't sound right, either. When I glance at him again, he's not even paying attention so I wait for her to return my text.

Are you sure you're not a comedian?

I make you laugh. I imagine her blushing, though knowing her, I'm probably pissing her off instead of making her want me.

I have to go. I don't want to get caught.

This strange fear comes out of hiding inside me, though I don't know what it's for. **Wait. Wha'cha doing today?**

School is out at three. Then I have FBLA.

Oh yeah, the future business leader. That should make me put my phone away right now, but instead I text her again. **Where do you go to school, future business leader?**

Remington Private in Cliffton.

Dude. Why doesn't it surprise me that she lives in Cliffton? It's like the Beverly Hills of our area. But then I remember how her skin felt beneath my hands and how she went from looking like the loneliest girl in the world to…I don't know, not so alone the longer I talked to her last night.

Let me come see you.

No reply.

Virginia, I text.

After another pause, I'm sitting here all jittery. It's fucking strange. Suddenly, I get a one-word reply.

Yes.

When school gets out, Shane and I head back over to his car. Drea, Tanner and Cody are already there waiting for us.

"Hey, can you drop me off in Cliffton?" I ask as Cody climbs into the backseat.

Shane looks at me over the car from where he stands at the

driver's side. "Yeah."

I see the wheels turning in his head. He knows I'm going to see the girl I was just texting.

"Cliffton?" He raises an eyebrow.

"Shut up."

Tanner climbs into the back with Cody and then Drea, and I sit up front.

"Who's in Cliffton?" Tanner asks as we drive.

"None of your business—ouch. Fucker." I rub the back of my head where he just thumped it.

We're quiet most of the way. I give him directions to her school after looking them up on my phone.

It doesn't take too long before Shane pulls up along the curb in front. There aren't many cars in the parking lot, and none of them are a piece of shit like Shane's.

"Dude," Shane starts but I cut him off, feeling strangely defensive.

"It's nothin'."

I get out of the car and then bend down to say goodbye. "Thanks, man. I'll catch you guys later." Reaching my hand out, I ruffle Drea's hair. "Don't let them get in any trouble without me."

She jerks her head out from under my hand.

What the? "Hey."

Drea smiles, and the tightness in my chest eases. "Have fun, Ry."

"Later." I stand, and slam the door closed behind me. My friends drive off and I shove my hands in my pockets, wondering what the hell I'm doing here.

Chapter Fifteen

Virginia

There once was a girl who didn't know her name. One day she found out it had been Lonely. It was the day she discovered that wasn't her anymore, and then she didn't know her name again.

~*~

Your school is fucking ridiculous.

After looking at Ryder's text, I shove my phone back into my pocket. There's a slow tingle in my chest as I think about him standing outside. I didn't expect him to come. Warning bells start sounding off in my mind, because I'm happy he's here. Really happy, and that's a dangerous thing.

I learned a long time ago not to put my happiness in someone else's hands because you can never trust them not to drop it. If Mom and Dad couldn't make it as a couple, no one can. I refuse to give up any part of myself to someone else, because no one should be responsible for me except for me. But then I remember how good it felt to talk to him, and how good it felt to kiss him, and how foreign those emotions had been before.

Not that I've never felt good or been happy, but it's always grown from my achievements and activities—school, FBLA, student council—not from another person. I'm not sure if that's a good thing or not.

"Lulu, what's going on?" Hailey whispers. We're working individually today, but Hailey and Jamie both sit beside me.

"What? Nothing."

Jamie's eyebrows pull together. "You're sitting there all smiley. You look like you're in la-la land or something."

Oh no. No, no, no, no. I shake my head as though that will make a difference. "I was just thinking." *And I was here, right here.* I'm not the girl who gets lost in her head.

"About what?" Jamie still eyes me as though she's trying to figure me out.

"Or *who?* Did Mike talk to you?" Hailey grins.

What? "Why would Mike talk to me?" I glance toward the other side of the room. Mike's scanning a piece of paper. Hailey and Jamie always tease me that Mike and I would make the perfect couple. We're number one and two in our class. He's involved in as many activities as I am. If I were to fall in love with a boy, it would be a boy like him. Grounded, stable, put together.

I swear Hailey bursts out of her skin with excitement. "He likes you. I'm not supposed to tell you. I promised him I wouldn't because he's going to, but, oh my God, Lu. He is so cute! I knew you were perfect for each other!"

My heart does this little jump thing, but as quickly as it happens, I take a deep breath and control it again. These are not the kind of things I get happy about. First Ryder and now Mike. I roll my eyes. "We are not perfect for each other." That's just not something I think is possible. "No, he didn't talk to me, but that's probably a good thing. It's senior year. I have much more important things to worry about than boys." Which is something I need to remember. What was I thinking telling Ryder he could come here?

"He's not just a boy. He's *Mike Dawson*. Seriously, Lu, if there were ever two people who could go out and not let it get in the way of their responsibilities, it's you and Mike." Jamie smiles at me. "That's why we've always said you two would be perfect together. You're both perfectionists. You both would rather be doing homework or working on student council than hanging out."

"You say that like you're not part of student council or don't get good grades." This isn't like Hailey and Jamie—to push something this way.

"No, but we balance it differently than you do, Lu. You have to admit that. When was the last time you hung out with us besides at school? I mean, you've always sort of been that way, but it feels different lately."

All kinds of excuses fumble around in my head: it's the beginning of the year, our *senior* year; I have a lot more responsibilities than they do; I'm going to *Stanford* next year.

None of my reasons come out, though; instead I listen as Hailey picks up where Jamie left off. "Not that we don't get it. Actually, we *don't* totally get it, but that's okay. You've always been more distant, but we just…it's our last year of high school. We should be having more fun."

She means *I* should be having more fun. And that makes me wonder what they've been doing without me. Things I know they would welcome me to participate in but probably didn't ask because they knew I'd say no.

There's nothing left in my chest now except loneliness; the

heavy weight of it making it hard for me to breathe. I'm lonely. Solitary. How could I have never realized how alone I feel?

"Let's hang out later. We can—"

"I can't," automatically comes out of my mouth, cutting Jamie off. She sighs. Guilt tumbles through me, but then I remember I really can't. Ryder is outside waiting for me.

Ryder. The guy with piercings in his lip, who curses like crazy and who can't possibly understand me. We're different, much too different. If Mike is perfect for me like Hailey and Jamie think, Ryder is one hundred percent wrong for me. We want different things, and we always will.

But kissing him didn't feel wrong. Listening to him talk didn't either.

"Over the weekend," I blurt out. It's a way to change the subject and stifle the thoughts in my head. "We should do something on the weekend. Have a sleepover and…I don't know…"

Loneliness is my heart disease, hardening my arteries and stopping my blood flow. I should know what I want to do. I'm seventeen years old. I shouldn't feel lost at the thought of going out and having a good time.

"Okay." Jamie gives me a hug.

"Should we invite Mike and his friends?" Hailey adds.

She hardly gets the words out before I'm shaking my head, though I don't know why. Because of my plan, or fear, or because of Ryder? There are too many variables. I just know I fear the emptiness inside me as much as I fear my destiny. I don't know how to change either one.

"I'm going to head out early, okay?" I push to my feet and place my stuff in my backpack. I tell Mr. Wave I need to leave because I have an appointment. It's only ten minutes early, and like Dad, he trusts me, so he tells me it's fine.

My head is cluttered, which makes the fear run deeper. Confusing, mixed-up thoughts always weigh me down. They make me feel like Mom, as though I'm not me or I don't have control. The thoughts make me wonder what Virginia Woolf felt like. If she always felt the heaviness of her life on her shoulders and in her head the way I do. Maybe she always felt so heavy that the rocks in her pocket didn't make a difference.

It's sprinkling when I get outside. Ryder's standing under the cover of the building with his head down, his hands shoved into his pockets. He's wearing long sleeves and jeans, but no jacket or hoodie again. My heart does this confusing *rap, rap, rap* but I shut it out of my mind. There are already too many thoughts there to decipher.

He glances up as though he heard me, and a smile tugs at his lips. "If it isn't the future business leader of America. Did you cut out early? I might have to tell on you."

Shaking my head, I step next to him, ignoring what he said. "You should be wearing a jacket."

"Aww, you're worried about me. That's so sweet."

I try not to smile, wondering how I can even want to right now. My head is a mess, and I can't handle messes. "You're crazy."

"And you're perfect, which if you ask me, is pretty, fucking crazy in itself."

His words are a slap across my face. "Ugh. Whatever. I'm not perfect."

I only get a step away before Ryder stops me with his body, standing in front of me. He has a wrinkle on his forehead and

92

questions in his multi-colored eyes. "I didn't mean that as a bad thing."

There's a gentleness to his voice I've never heard before. Somehow, the edge is still there, but muted. "I know." And I do, though I don't know how. "Let's go."

Ryder moves out of my way as I turn for my car. He's walking next to me, and a strange thought adds to the madness in my head: what would Hailey and Jamie think if they saw us together?

Ryder isn't like Mike.

"Where are we going?" he asks, and I answer with the only thing I can.

"To do homework."

Chapter Sixteen

Ryder

Homework definitely isn't what I expected to be doing with her when I had Shane drop me off. It's not something I expect to do most of the time.

Virginia's walking like some creepy guy is behind her while she's on a quiet street at night, so I don't say anything until we get to the car. When we get there, I look at her from over the top of it, her eyes catching mine as she opens the door. "I can call Shane to come back and get me if you don't wanna chill." Because I'm suddenly wondering if I'm who she's trying to escape. Yeah, she told me to come here, but I'm not stupid. I realize that at any second she could decide that hanging out with me is too fucked up. That we're too different. Hell, I might decide the same thing.

"No...I...I wouldn't have said to come if that's not what I wanted."

Those words somehow knock the breath out of me. I'm usually pretty good at understanding how the world works. I get that Luke doesn't want to be stuck with me. Shit like that happens. I understand that Dad had to leave. Yeah, the things he does are wrong, and no, I shouldn't do them; but there's a balance to the world—people like Virginia and Luke who are smart and have plans, and people like me who aren't all that good. We give people like them something to aspire to be better than, and something to rebel against. Give people like Mr. Miller someone to try and control.

We can't all be future business leaders of America.

We can't all be perfect.

Even if I wanted to, I wouldn't know the first way to try.

But with Virginia, I don't totally get how she works. She shouldn't be here with me, yet she is. She shouldn't have been out there on the dock, yet she was. She shouldn't care if I wear a jacket or do things like give me her number for a ride or bring me my hoodie, but she did.

She's supposed to assume the worst with me, which I guess really means just seeing me as I am, because I don't try and hide it.

So right now, what I'm feeling is curiosity.

But then her eyes cast down, her body slumps like her bones aren't working, and she reminds me of the girl who climbed out on that dock.

"I know this isn't your idea of a good time," Virginia says. "If you want to go, go, but I just…I need to clear my head. I need something that has a straightforward answer—question and answer. Homework is so much easier than life."

Her body stiffens again and she looks at me, all strength, and I realize I'm a liar. It's not only curiosity that has me here. She's not just a compulsion, either. I see something in her that's lost—lost the same way Shane and Drea are. Like Tanner and Cody.

Like me. And for the first time in my life, I want to try and lead someone out of it. Not that I wouldn't change things for my friends if I could, but the rest of us, we sort of belong where we are. We fit. She doesn't.

"Yeah...yeah, okay, boss. Let's go."

Her lips sort of pucker like she didn't expect what I said, but then she nods and gets into the car. I do the same. We hardly make it out of the parking lot before the rain starts coming down harder, splats of water smearing across her windshield. "Guess this leaves out Ghetto Beach. We could sit in your car, but I might suffocate. I mean, really, a Prius?"

"Hey! It's not that bad."

"It's small. This thing is a fucking deathtrap if you get into an accident."

"I like it. It makes sense. It's good for the environment and good on gas."

Why am I not surprised at how she answered? "We can head somewhere close to my place."

"No. Too far. My dad's at work late tonight. We'll go to my house."

"Cool." I hit the button so the seat leans back. I drum my fingers on my thighs as Virginia drives. Her house isn't too far away from her school. The second we pull up, I realize this was a huge fucking mistake. I should have known her house would be just as ridiculous as her school.

This is the kind of place Dad would eye and see dollar signs. It's the kind of place I feel the urge to do the same thing.

I never did private homes with him, but I know he took them. My skin gets tight just looking at the huge, white house in front of me. It's different than going into Tanner's place, because, rich kid or not—and knowing Tanner probably has more of a future than any of us—it's still like looking in the mirror when I see him. With her, I know eventually she won't be lost anymore.

Those words become a noose tied around my neck. Not too tight, just letting me know they're there. This girl has become kind of a friend. I can't sit here and think about stealing from her.

"I'm not going in there." This whole thing, being with her at all, is stupid. I reach for the handle, but Virginia's hand on my other arm makes me pause.

"You don't want me in there," I add when she doesn't speak.

"Yes, I do. I don't get it. I don't know why, and that's…I don't work that way, Ryder. I need things to make sense or I feel like I'm losing it. I'm not stupid. I'm not the girl who dreams about her 'happily ever after' with a boy. It's not something I've ever wanted. I'm far too practical for that, but…I guess when I'm with you, I can pretend it's okay to want something different. I've never really wanted something like that before."

It's crazy how I can make a girl like this want something. And not like the rich girls who show up at our parties sometimes. She doesn't want to pass the time with me just to say she took a visit to the other side of the tracks, or to piss off her parents.

Or hell, maybe that's exactly what she wants. But if she's going to pretend, I can, too, because that's what we're doing. She's destined to be one kind of person, and I'm destined to be another. The kind who looks at a house like this and doesn't think of the lonely girl inside, unless it's what he can take from her.

Chapter Seventeen

Virginia

Standing in my bedroom, I suddenly feel like I'm on a boat. My stomach is doing this swish thing, like I'm rocking back and forth on waves and might have to stick my head over the edge to vomit at any second.

Dramatic, I know, but it's true.

I've never had a boy in my room before. I've definitely never had a boy like Ryder anywhere near my bedroom before.

I watch him as he walks across the carpet. Mocha is the color. I know because I'm the one who picked it out.

His pants are baggy but not *too* big. I can tell that the tip of his underwear probably shows at the top. It's not something I've ever been into. I mean, why not just buy pants that fit, right? But for some reason, I like it on him. Like Ryder doesn't care about rules the way I do. Like he's different. Different colors flash in my head and I wonder what type they are. Boxers or briefs? And then I realize I sound like a total perv, the heat of my face telling me it's probably changing to multiple shades of red.

"You're blushing," Ryder says.

"No I'm not." I've become quite the liar lately.

"Okay." He turns his back to me. Ryder runs his finger along the edge of my bookshelf. "You have a ton of books. You're like the perfect good girl. You do your homework on time and you read lots of books. My brother is just like that."

Yes, that's me. My name is Perfect... Though it's really not.

"Is that what you like to do for fun? Read?" Ryder leaves the bookshelf now, but continues to make his way around my room, looking at everything. He touches the jewelry box Mom got me that rests on my dresser. Picks up a magazine that's open to an article on one of my favorite mathematicians. He stops by the shelf on the wall, studying all of my trophies and awards—FBLA, government, and the one I got for helping teach elementary kids at the youth center about different jobs in business they could have one day.

My eyes dart to the bookshelf and back to Ryder. He's not looking at me, but I'm suddenly wishing he was. I want to know what he's thinking when he looks at my things. What it tells him about me, because his question somehow told me something about myself.

I like to read... And not because I have to do it for school, but because I enjoy it. I tell myself I don't. I want to believe I don't, because reading is like a fresh wound for me, one that never heals. It's tied in with writing and Mom and Grandma and living in imaginary worlds instead of being rooted in reality. "No." I shake my head. "Books are Mom's thing, not mine. She just always buys them for me."

My backpack drops silently to my bed before I unzip it and start pulling my binder and schoolbooks out. "Do you want something to drink? I have Diet Dr. Pepper."

There's no reply, but I hear his footsteps on the mocha carpet, heading my way. A warm body stops right behind me, close enough to feel his heat and smell his soapy skin. "Nothing about you makes sense."

I flinch when fingers touch my hair. My eyes fall closed when he slides a lock behind my ear.

No, no, no, Lulu. Step away. Hanging out is one thing, but don't fall under his spell.

My eyes jerk open. "You're awesome at compliments. Every girl wants to be told she doesn't make sense."

"See, like that. You don't give a shit what some random guy says about you. You probably don't care what anyone says. You're too level-headed for that, so why do you pretend you do?"

That's where he's wrong. I don't want to care what people say or think, especially a boy—or maybe just this boy—but I do. For the first time in my life I wonder if that's something all girls care about, whether they want to admit it or not, or if I'm just not the kind of girl I thought I was. Or the kind of girl I want to be, at least when it comes to boys.

"There are pens and pencils at my desk if you need one. I usually do my homework on my bed." Yes, I'm aware that I changed the subject rather than answering him. *There once was a girl named Fear...*

"Rebel."

"Comedian."

Using my left foot, I hold my right shoe so I can pull my foot out, and then do the same with the other. After lining them up straight, I climb onto my bed. My lap desk is beside me because I put it on my bed after making it this morning. Things go much easier when you're prepared.

I set my desk over my lap and my notebook and pen on the desk. Already some of the tension starts to ease out of my body as I finger through my math book.

"Holy shit, this is so strange." Ryder takes his shoes off, too, and then sits on the bed beside me. He doesn't straighten his shoes out.

"What's strange?" I tried not to ask him, really, I did. It shouldn't matter. But this is the second time he's said something about us is strange.

"Nothin'."

Whatever. I start my first calculus problem. I smell his soap again. Instead of working, he fingers the leather bracelet on his wrist.

"So, what *do* you do?" Ryder asks a few minutes later.

Without looking at him, I reply, "Do?"

"For fun."

Don't look his way. If you do, you'll stop working, and that's not what you came here for. It's not what you need. "FBLA. I'm also president of student council. I do some volunteering. Oh, and I'm organizing this fundraiser for school where—"

"I said for fun."

I slap the pencil down on the desk and jerk my head his way. "That *is* fun for me. Would it be cooler if I said partying and bonfires on the beach?"

"Maybe a little." Ryder holds up his hand, his fingers open about an inch. He's smiling, but it looks almost fake. His eyes glance my way, and then around my room, then down, and I realize he's not being a jerk, he's uncomfortable. Out of his element. Unsure.

I wonder if this is the first time he's felt something like that. Ryder doesn't strike me as the kind of guy who feels insecure often.

"We came here to do homework, remember?"

"No, *you* came here to do homework. I came because you're beautiful."

And... there goes my blush again.

Tit for tat. He's nervous so he's trying to do the same to me. "Hand me your backpack."

"Yes, boss."

"That's the second time you've called me that. Why?"

"Because you're a future business leader of America, remember? And you're bossy." He winks his blue eye at me.

My elbow makes contact with his side and he groans even though I know it wasn't hard enough for it to hurt. "I'm not bossy. I'm self-assured. Hand me your bag."

Ryder raises a brow. Okay, so I'm a little bossy.

He hands me his backpack and I eye him as if to ask if I can open it. He nods and I pull out an Algebra book with a piece of paper stuffed inside. "Come on, we'll do yours first."

And then I set my table on the floor, lie on my stomach and set his work out in front of me. Ryder pauses, waits so long that I'm not sure he's going to move, but then finally he stretches out next to me.

For the next hour, we do his homework together. He's a little confused by the equations so I explain some of the formulas. The longer I talk, the more I expect him to tell me to shut up and that he doesn't give a crap about this, but he doesn't. He actually listens.

After he finishes the last problem, I feel his eyes on me, trying to look inside me. "Your eyes scrunch up right here when you're concentrating." He rubs his thumb against the side of my forehead beside my eyes, which are now drifting closed.

"I wanna kiss you again, Virginia. That's it. Just kiss."

It's as though he knows I needed to hear that last part. I open my eyes and turn his way. I'm mid-nod when his lips capture mine. They're softer, gentler than they were the first time. He brushes his thumb over the same spot he previously touched before pushing his hand through my hair. He rolls me over, but doesn't lie on me like he did at the beach. Just leans over me, pressing tender kisses to my mouth. Exploring it with his tongue as though it's a foreign land that he's just discovered.

"My head is wrinkling your paper," I say when his mouth moves to my neck.

Ryder chuckles against the skin there. "I don't care."

We kiss some more. Kiss so much my lips feel raw but I don't care. Soon, my hand is on his chest like it was at the beach, and I'm easing him away. "My Dad will be back soon. I should get you home."

But I don't want to. He gazes down at me. I don't want him to leave, and I don't want to know what that means, either. Because if I do, my name will change to Fear again, and I'll run.

Chapter Eighteen

Ryder

She's quiet while I pack up all my stuff. There's this thought bearing down on my brain, and I wonder if I shouldn't have kissed her again. Maybe it was the wrong thing to do. She obviously has some shit going on, and she needs to clear her head, yet I decide it's the best time to make out with her.

I feel all upside down and backward with her. It's easier to use my mouth on her sometimes rather than trying to figure out what to say, or how to say it. Not that I don't want to kiss her, because yeah, I definitely want that, but it's like I'm trying to find my way through a maze when I'm with her. She's always surprising me, and I'm not used to that. I don't know how to navigate it.

That shit with the homework. I don't know why it's got me on edge but it does. My friends never would have cracked open a book with me (not that I would have with them, either). Luke would have made me feel stupid about it, like I'm not smart enough to work on my own or that I don't know what I should be doing.

It wasn't like that with Virginia.

I can't figure out why that matters.

The quiet continues on the drive to my house. The word sorry teases my tongue but I can't make it come out. I don't really do that—apologize. Not typically. And I also don't know if I have something to apologize for.

She pulls up in front of my shitty house and I sit there for a minute. This is ridiculous. I'm being lame. If I want to say something, all I need to do is open my mouth. I've never been like this, and it's all kinds of screwed up. "I never got that before. The math."

Totally not what I expected to say.

"Yeah?" she asks, excitement making her voice go up a notch, and suddenly I'm glad those were the words I spoke.

"I never cared before. I don't know if I do now, but…thanks. For not talking to me like I'm stupid, or pushing me into it. I guess thanks for not assuming homework's not something I would do, either."

Her lips spread into a huge smile. It's like she's letting me in for the first time. She's laughed and smiled before, but not at me. Not like this.

"But I wouldn't… Have done it. You should probably know that. I can pretty much guarantee I wouldn't have done my work today if I hadn't been with you." She should know who she's with. There isn't anything about me that is like her. I don't want to lie to her about that. *Then why haven't you told her everything? That my eyes cased her house when I walked in, thinking of all the money in it.*

"I guess it's good that you were with me then. And maybe…" She tilts her head down. My hand suddenly has a mind of its own and slides under her chin, lifting slowly until she's looking me in the eyes again.

Just as I'm about to ask her, maybe what, she takes a deep breath and speaks. "Maybe you'll have to be with me more often so we can make sure you keep it up."

That's my girl. There's fear in her eyes, fear of what she said and probably of saying it, but she did it anyway. It doesn't surprise me. I see how strong she is. Earlier, I thought she was the kind of girl Dad would take advantage of, but I was wrong. She would never allow something like that to happen.

"It's my eyes, isn't it? The colors get girls every time. Either that, or the piercings."

Virginia shakes her head, but I can tell she wants to grin at what I said. We both need to steer clear of the topic of fear, though. Even though I've never really been scared of anything in my life, I bet my eyes reflect hers. I've never wanted to be with someone the way I find myself wanting to be with her, and that, ladies and gentlemen, is scary as fuck.

"See ya later, boss lady." I let my hand run down the side of her face, and then I get out. When I make it to my front door, I turn toward her car. It's not until then that she drives away.

It's not until then that I realize something else, too.

I feel *good*.

And not the way I typically do. Not because I'm high or spent the day having fun with my friends. I can't explain it. I just feel *good*, in the same way I would when Dad looked at me with pride in his eyes, or when I was like eleven and Luke hung out with me all day. He took me to the park and we got ice cream bars. Neither of us had money, and I told him I'd steal them, but he told me he didn't want that for me. It made me feel like he thought I might be good at something besides stealing, and it made me feel awesome all day.

We made a fort in his room that night, which he was totally too old for. We stayed up late watching movies. It was like three a.m. when he pulled this book out from under the bed. It was a book about all the states and what each of them was known for. He told me all the places he wanted to go. That was the first time I realized Luke wanted to leave me. He never once mentioned me going with him. That's when I decided I couldn't afford to need him. He saw me just like he did Dad.

The door sticks a little when I push it open. My forehead wrinkles when I see Mr. Perfect in the kitchen. He was supposed to be at work tonight.

"I made homemade pizza bread. Remember when we used to do that? We'd eat them every night for like a week straight." Luke pops one of his knuckles.

"Huh?" We don't sit down to dinner together. We don't make pizza bread together anymore.

"Funny. It's dinner. Let's eat." He nods toward the table, and then goes to the fridge. "Are you home for the night?"

"Yeah." I head for the kitchen.

"Want a beer?"

"Excuse me, what? Didn't you just give me shit the other day for drinking?"

Luke sighs. He's standing by the open fridge. It's old and yellow and makes too loud a noise. "I'm trying here, Ry. Do you want a drink or not?"

I glance at the door, half expecting a TV show to bust in and say this is all a big joke or something. When nothing happens, I nod. "Yeah. Cool. Thanks. I'll grab the plates."

Luke takes two beers out of the fridge while I take two plates from the cabinet. I toss a couple pizza breads on each of them and set them on the table. He sits first, then eyes me and the chair, before I join him.

"You need a new hoodie," he says before taking a bite. I finish chewing what's in my mouth before replying.

"Yeah."

"We'll get you another one."

Okay, what's going on here? He's supposed to be telling me how irresponsible I am and that he doesn't have the money to buy stuff like that. "You don't have to. Tanner's closet is as big as my bedroom. He said he'll give me one."

"That's nice of him. What are they up to? Your friends? They haven't been around much lately." I don't know why, but I get this light, almost floaty feeling in my chest as he speaks to me like this, all normal and shit. Like brothers.

"Same, I guess. Tan and Cody are attached at the lips like always. Shane's worried about his mom. He thinks she's using again."

Luke curses. "Tell him to come crash on the couch. There's always room for him."

The sensation in my chest expands at that. Luke doesn't think much of my friends, but he's cool to them, and that means a lot to me.

"What about you and Drea?"

I roll my eyes. "There is no me and Drea." He's always thought that, no matter how many times I've said we're only friends. Friends who mess around sometimes, but friends all the same. "She's doing okay, though. She hasn't really said much."

Luke takes a bite of his pizza, chews and swallows, and then takes another one. We don't talk as we both eat, and I have to admit, it's pretty cool. Just chilling with him.

When his food is gone, he leans back in his chair and says, "I got a call from your principal today. He said you didn't do your homework and you skipped your last couple classes. You can't do that anymore, Ry. You need to get serious."

The lightness is gone, replaced by a heavy weight in my chest. It won't matter if I tell him I did my work. Hell, I could even show him, but I won't. Can't he trust me? Ask for my side before automatically giving me shit?

That's not what has me feeling like I want to burst out of my own skin, though. He didn't want to hang out with me tonight. This dinner was a screwed up ploy before he opened his mouth to tell me how much of a disappointment I am. Just like that day when I was eleven, he made me think one thing just so he could drop a bomb on me. The worst part is, he took away the satisfaction I felt from my afternoon with Virginia.

"Why does it matter? We both know I'm destined to be just like Dad anyway."

Luke groans. Without another word, I get up and go to my room.

Chapter Nineteen

Virginia

I've talked to Ryder every day since we did homework at my house. It's only been a few days, but still. I'm not sure what it means, and, honestly, it's easier not thinking about it. That's probably not healthy, but I decide not to think about that, either.

It's Friday, my sleepover with Hailey and Jamie. We used to do this way more often than we do now. It's strange how sometimes things like that stop or slow down and you don't really have a reason why. They're still my best friends, and I know I'm still theirs, but I haven't been showing it the way I should. Tonight is about changing that. Even though they don't know it, they've kept me sane when I've felt like falling apart.

"Do you realize we've eaten pizza, popcorn and ice cream all in one night? I feel like I'm going to explode." Hailey puts a pale hand on her stomach, her blonde hair fanning out on my bed.

My phone buzzes. When I glance over, I see it says Mom again and I ignore it.

"I was about to ask Lulu if she had any chips." Jamie grins, and I know she's probably telling the truth. She's always been able to eat what she wants and not gain weight. She's also the most active of us all. She's played sports all her life, and has a toned body to show for it.

"I hate you." Hailey grabs a pillow and hits her with it, making us all laugh.

I watch them for a second. Both of my friends are gorgeous—Jamie the athlete, with her perfect dark skin and gorgeous hair, and Hailey, the angel.

Out of nowhere, I wonder what Ryder would think of them. If he would like Hailey's platinum hair or Jamie's exotic look. It's never been something I've worried about before, but I suddenly feel very plain.

Ugh. Stop it, Lu. You don't care about things like that.

"Did you turn in the proposal I gave you to the principal about installing new showerheads in the locker rooms? Fixing them over and over doesn't seem to work."

"Of course." Jamie wrinkles her nose as if to say, *duh,* and I realize she's right. Neither of them has ever dropped the ball on something so important. I don't know why I even asked.

"That's enough about that." Hailey moves into a sitting position so the three of us are facing each other. "No talking about school tonight—at least not traditional school things. This is our senior year. We should be having more fun than we are. It's not like the three of us can't keep up our school activities and have more of a social life."

They look at me, and I know that *the three of us* really means *me.*

Again, Ryder climbs into my thoughts. *Go away, go away, go away.*

"Yeah, for once let's pretend to be normal seventeen-year-old girls." Jamie winks.

The word *normal* echoes, my inner voice repeating it over

and over as if I'm standing in the middle of nowhere. "Caring about showers is normal."

"You know what she means, Lu." Hailey sets her hand on my leg. "So…Mike? Have you put any more thought into him? Homecoming is next month…Everyone knows the two of you will probably win king and queen anyway…"

"Juan totally asked her!" Jamie blurts out, and Hailey slaps her arm. "I can't help it! It just happened today."

Juan is Mike's best friend. I see where she's going with this now, and an uncomfortable twist turns my stomach. We go to all the dances because we help plan most of them. We've always had a rule for dances—either we all go with a date, or we all go alone. "What did you say?"

"I told him I'd get back to him." She glances down. Hailey wants to go with him. That much is obvious.

"What about you?" I take in Jamie next, but she's already shaking her head.

"No one has asked yet."

"Rumor has it that Danny is asking her, though. It's still early. I'm surprised Juan already asked me."

And, of course, Danny is close with Juan and Mike as well. I'm seeing a pattern here. "You guys should totally go." I mean that. It is our senior year, and I don't want them to miss out.

"It's not like Mike isn't going to ask you. We'll all go together."

The twist is back, tying my belly into knots. Ryder isn't the kind of boy to go to a dance with me. I don't even know if I want him to, or if I *should* want him to.

I have a feeling kissing like we have isn't a huge deal to him. I know he's done more. He doesn't have to tell me that for me to know it.

In a month's time, I'm sure he'll be done with me—or I'll be done with him. It's not like either of us is looking for that high school sweetheart you see in all the books and movies.

But the thought of going with Mike feels wrong.

I shake my head. "He hasn't asked. He might not."

"He will." Hailey looks confused, as if this is a no-brainer.

"You don't want to go with him?" Jamie asks.

I have two choices here. I can lie to them or tell them the truth. As dishonest as I've been lately, I'm not really a liar. I despise lying. There's never been a time that I lied to my best friends. Not telling them about Mom isn't a lie, really. It's just keeping some things for myself.

My shoulders lift and fall in a shrug. "There's sort of this guy…"

"Oh my God!" Jamie shouts.

"It's not serious!" I grab both their wrists so they don't start dancing around and celebrating something that isn't real. "He goes to a different school. We just sort of met, and like I said, it's not a big deal. You guys know I've always said I refuse to get serious about anyone until after college. It feels weird to think about someone else, though, ya know? Honestly, there's a possibility we won't even be talking by the time Homecoming comes around."

An unpleasant shiver shakes my insides.

"What does he look like?"

"What's his name?"

"Where did you meet?" They start rapid-firing questions at me in a pace that takes my breath away, let alone allows me to answer them. "Umm…" This should not feel as totally weird as it does. We've never really done this before, though. Yeah, we've dated, but none of us have ever really been crazy about boys. "One of his eyes is blue and the other is part blue and part brown. And Ryder."

"*Ride her*?" Jamie giggles. "What does that mean? I mean, besides the obvious."

"What!" This time it's my turn to hit her with the pillow. "Not *ride her*. His name. It's Ryder."

"What school does he go to? What about college? I bet he's going to Stanford next year, too, and *you,* the one of us who is the most anti-boy, will fall in love and go off to college with your boyfriend at the end of the year." Hailey looks like she's floating and I wonder why I didn't realize there's a closet romantic in her.

Once the thought settles in, something else hits me. Does Ryder want to go to college? Does he know where he's going? What does he want to do with his life? I don't really know much about him at all…so why does it feel like I do? Maybe more importantly, why am I not losing it over that?

"That isn't even close to a possibility." I shrug. "And I wouldn't want it to be, either." I don't even know if Ryder *wants* to go to college. He's not the type of boy who would be what Hailey just described, though, and I'm not that girl, either. "Let's go get some chips and dip now."

Jamie and Hailey share a look I don't understand. Thankfully, they drop the subject. We go downstairs and pig out again. Dad teases us, and Jamie asks him what kind of cases he's working on.

Afterward, we head back upstairs, watch a movie and then talk and laugh some more. Every time they toss more Ryder questions at me, I deflect them.

A couple hours later, my friends are asleep on an air mattress on my floor.

My eyes haven't closed except to blink. My stomach is heavy. My whole body is.

Without letting myself think, I grab my phone and listen to the voicemail from earlier.

Virginia... It's Mom. I guess you know that, right? You can't keep doing this, kiddo. You can't keep ignoring me, and...and you can't keep hating me. I know it wasn't always easy on you. I also know all of that isn't something I can blame on my Dissociative Identity Disorder. I know I've never really been the kind of mom you need, but I do love you. I've always loved you.

"I love you, too," I whisper.

With tears in my eyes, I delete the message.

There once was a girl named Guilt...

Chapter Twenty

Ryder

"Can you drop me off in Cliffton again?" I ask Shane.

It's Saturday afternoon and we were going out to get food. Virginia texted me to see if I want to go over and do homework. Home-fucking-work. On a Saturday. Who does that? And more importantly, why do I want to go?

"You got gas money, Romeo?" he replies.

"Funny."

"Do you want my car? It's not like I ever drive it." Tanner leans forward from the backseat.

"You're so screwed up." I glance back at him. "Who the hell gets a brand new Beamer and doesn't drive it?" I get it though. His parents want him to be someone he's not. They want him to be the kind of guy who wants to go to the private schools they like. Taking the car means he's willing to be that person.

"Take him to Cliffton. I have cash." Tanner leans back again.

"No. You're not paying for my shit. I have a few bucks.

We're good." I toss a handful of crumpled-up bills at Shane. Luke doesn't let me have much money. Not that he has very much. But he's scared of what I'll spend it on. I'm surprised he even left me that. Probably a peace offering after the other day. We haven't talked since.

Drea's quiet, playing with the bracelet on her wrist as we drive. I've never seen it before, and briefly, I wonder where she got it.

I give Shane directions to Virginia's house. Her dad is apparently off meeting with a client. I don't know what he does, and I'm not sure I want to.

When we pull up out front, all of my friends are silent.

"Holy shit. You're screwing someone who lives in *that* house?" Shane sounds in awe.

"I'm not having sex with her." I reach around Drea and shove him. "And shut up. Don't bring it up again."

Reaching for the handle, I open it. It was stupid of me to bring them here. It's not like they'll understand. I don't even understand what's going on.

A hand on my arm stops me as I'm halfway out of the car. I turn to look at Drea. "What are you doing, Ry? You don't belong in there. You don't *want* to belong in there."

Her words bounce around my head. She's right. I don't belong here. I know it, she knows it, Virginia knows it. Everyone in the car does, too. Virginia will always belong here, and I never will. That's just the way life is.

It's the other part that makes my hand start to tremble on the door handle, because for the first time in my life, a feeling I'm not familiar with comes out of hiding. I think I might want to belong in a place like this. Or at least be accepted here. Because

I never would be. Drea's reaction proves that. There isn't a question in my mind that Virginia's parents would freak if they met me.

I know she has an expensive-looking vase on a table behind the door. A glass cabinet full of expensive china. Those aren't the only things I eyed. I'm my dad after all.

"Just havin' a little fun, Dre." After I finish sliding out of the car, I wink at her. "You guys partying tonight?"

"Yep. Bonfire. You going?" Cody asks. He doesn't typically talk much unless it's to answer a question or speak to Tanner, so I'm sort of surprised.

"Yeah. I'll make it out." With each step I take away from the car, I try to shove my thoughts out of my head. There has never been a time in my life I wanted more than I have, and there's no reason to start now. Luke's the one who turned his back on who we are. Not me.

As soon as I make it to the door, it's opening. Virginia is standing there in a pair of nice blue jeans and a sweatshirt. I like that about her. Most rich girls I've seen always dress the part, but she seems like she goes more for comfort.

"Wanted to make out with me again?" I lean against the doorjamb and cross my arms.

She rolls her eyes. "Wanted to do *homework* with you again."

"Excuse." I step closer, put my finger under her chin and tilt her head up. My lips touch hers, and I don't rush this time. Just give her a few closed-mouth kisses before I taste her. There's mint on her tongue, like she just brushed her teeth, mixing with her ocean scent.

A thought slams into my brain, making me jerk back. "Fuck. Your dad already left, right?" The last thing I want is an angry, rich father after me.

Virginia laughs. "Of course. I wouldn't have invited you over if he was still here."

Oh. I step back. It's not something I didn't know. Just a minute ago the thought went through my head, but it's different hearing it from her lips.

"No." Her expressive, green eyes go wide. "That's not what I meant."

But it is. "Yeah, it was. But it's cool." Shrugging my shoulders, I try to step around her. Virginia touches my arm, and that's all it takes for me to stop.

"It's not. I'm not like that. I've gone out with boys before, and I've never introduced any of them to my father. The only ones he's met are guys I've gone to a dance with, because he sort of *has* to meet them. It's not *you*. I just don't do that. Introduce a guy to my family."

For some reason, I'm not sure that makes me feel any better. "It's cool."

Her hand slides down my arm, one of her fingers latching with mine. She won't look at me, though. "I want you here. That's a big thing for me to admit. I had a hard night last night. I couldn't concentrate today when I really needed to."

It's like what she said last time I came over, I think. When she needed to do her work to clear her head. I think it levels her—gives her stability she needs, for some reason. It doesn't make sense why she would call me here for that. It has to be easier without me, but I'm not going to argue with her about it, because the truth is I want to be here as well.

"Come on." I don't let go of her hand. She uses the other one to close the door before I lead her up the stairs. My feet follow the same path from the other day as I walk to her bedroom.

When we get there, our hands part. She closes the door and I kick out of my shoes. She's not wearing any. It's me who sits on her bed first, but Virginia is right behind me. She already has her books out, but she lifts the small table to her lap as she settles in.

"What about you?" she asks.

"Don't have it with me. I'll watch."

"Oh, we don't have to, then. We can go get yours and—"

"Just work, Virginia. It's okay."

So she does. She starts writing out problems and finding their answers. I lie down beside her and watch her work—watch the lines of concentration in her forehead. Watch her little frowns as she solves a problem. Watch when she chews her nail, which shocks me. It's something I bet she only does when she's lost in work, because I can tell they're manicured.

She keeps busy for over an hour without speaking, and I let her do her thing. At one point, she pushes the sleeves of her sweatshirt up. I reach out and let my fingers brush up and down her arm. She flinches, but then relaxes...and doesn't pull away.

"I don't want to distract you," I tell her.

"You're okay..."

So I don't stop touching her. Her skin is warm and soft. I'm not sure why there's the need to feel her all the time; maybe it's because I'm not sure why she's really here with me. I brush her arm and watch the little hairs there stand. I push a lock of hair behind her ear. My finger rubs the round diamond in her lobe, which I have no doubt is real. When she smiles, I touch her dimple and she shivers. Okay, that's probably too much, so I drop my hand to her arm again, this time just resting it there. Just touching. I didn't realize I needed this kind of contact before her.

Virginia keeps working, from one subject to the other. She couldn't concentrate before, I remind myself. Somehow, I'm doing something for her. Me. Ryder, the guy who has two strikes, is good at stealing, and whose brother hates him. But for her, I do something.

I think I have a girlfriend... Not someone I mess around with and not a friend with benefits. A girlfriend.

And I think I like it, too.

Chapter Twenty-One

Virginia

He hasn't kept his hands off me the whole time I've been doing my homework. It's different from the other times he's touched me. Where before it was sexual, this time it's just...touch. That's the only way I know how to explain it, though I don't know if that makes any sense.

It makes my blood run faster through my veins and my heart thump harder, but I'm somehow relaxed as well. I've sat here doing homework, clearing my head, which is something I struggled with before Ryder came over. I question if that's a good thing or not.

"Finished." I close my last book and set it on the floor.

"Do you get straight A's?" he asks, looking up at me from his spot on the bed.

"Yes."

"I knew the answer to that. Don't even know why I asked. I don't, Virginia. I'm not into school like you are. That's not who I am." His voice holds a hint of vulnerability that sounds so out of place there. He's cocky, and has a bad mouth.

"So?" It's funny how a few weeks ago I never would have

imagined myself using that word after what he said—coming from anyone, not just a boy. But he wouldn't be here right now if he was a different kind of boy. I see that.

"It's not that I don't want you to do well. School is important. I think you *can* do well, but..." But what? I like the edge in him? I shouldn't. That's a very bad thing. And it makes me feel selfish. "We'll do your work next time, too. I mean, not if you don't want to. I'm not trying to push you, and it's not that I don't think you can do it on your own, but—"

"Shh." He presses a finger to my lips. "It's not that I don't think you're cute as hell when you ramble, but I know what you meant. You don't make me feel like I'm not good enough, which is kind of fucked up and unexpected, but it's true."

The sadness in his voice makes me wonder if *he* thinks he's not good enough. It makes me wonder who else makes Ryder feel that way. And I can't help but think that if I had met him on a different night of my life, I might have thought the same thing.

Electricity zaps at my nerve endings as I lean down. As I press my lips to his for the first time. It's a quick kiss, and my face is on fire, but I'm glad I did it. "Do you want some Diet Dr. Pepper? I'm thirsty." My body practically bounces out of the bed I move so quickly.

And there it is. His cocky smile. He has his arms behind his head, grinning, because he knows I'm embarrassed. The jerk.

"I'm okay. Thanks, though."

"I'll get you one anyway. I'll be right back!" I nearly stumble, I take the stairs so quickly. When I make it to the kitchen, I suck in a deep breath. There's a good chance it's the first one I've taken since I kissed him.

I just finish pouring two cups of Diet Dr. Pepper when the front door opens and closes. *Oh no.*

Halfway there, I run into who just came in, and it's not Dad, it's Mom.

"I can't do this, Virginia. I tried and tried to give you your space, but I can't do it anymore!" She sounds slightly panicked. Not in real freak-out mode, but it could get there quickly.

My pulse is going so fast, it makes my chest hurt. My eyes dart up the stairs. I left my door open. "You have to go. I can't do this right now, Mom." Did I speak quietly enough?

"No, I can't do that anymore. Look, I'm sorry for everything you've had to deal with because of me. I know it's not easy, baby girl, and I know I've hurt you, but what you're doing—pretending none if this is happening—it's not healthy. I spoke to my psychiatrist and—"

"Mom!" This time I do scream. It's the only way to make her hear me. "Let's go outside." But then…what if the neighbors hear?

She's in that place where she can't hear a word I'm saying, though. Her mind works overtime. It's always been like that. She's pacing in front of me and running a hand through her hair. "You won't write. You won't write because of me. I know about the young writer competition. Your teacher wants you to do it. She thinks you have a chance to win. You're good, and you like it. I know you do. Don't run from your talent because it makes you feel closer to me."

I flinch, her words hitting me in the chest. She knows. I didn't realize she knew what scares me about it. That my biggest fear is being like her. But then I'm angry, too. How does she know what I like? What I want? "Stop trying to turn me into you! Maybe I hate it. Maybe I want nothing to do with giving my life to people who don't exist! I just want to be normal." My eyes are burning now, and my face is wet. I'm crying. I can't even remember the last time I cried in front of her, and I hate it. Tears make me feel weak.

That's when I see the flip in her. Her emotions have always run high. She has a fiery temper. Not that she would ever hurt me, because she wouldn't, but she's angry, and Mom doesn't believe in holding back how you feel. "Don't do that to me. It's not fair. Don't you dare tell me I am not normal. I'm still your mother, and you need to respect me. My DID is not my fault."

I know that. I do. I think. But… "It's not mine, either!" Yet, it still hurts me. It hurts me all the time. "How do I even know you're *you* right now! I can't ever trust you. I never know who you are." No one can understand what that's like. To know that at any moment, your mom can become someone else. Someone who hates you or doesn't want you. To need her so badly, only to see her look at you with disgust and say, *ugh, it's you again.* Still, my words have hurt her. I can see the pain reflecting in her eyes as if I have struck her.

Mom pauses for a moment, wipes her eyes, gives me a sad smile and then walks out. I want to follow her and say I'm sorry. I want what I said not to be true. I want to run away so I don't have to face Ryder.

But I don't. Instead, I wipe my eyes, clear my throat and walk up the stairs. When I get to the landing, I see him standing in my doorway, hands in his pockets.

"I don't want to talk about it."

I go to walk past him, but his right arm shoots out, blocking the doorway. "I know." Then he wraps that arm around me and pulls me to him.

And I let him.

He runs his hand through my hair, holding me against him, tightly.

And I let him do that, too.

He had to have heard everything; I have no doubt about that, but he doesn't ask. He's the only person I know who wouldn't ask. Ryder just holds me. I breathe him in. My eyes start to water again but I don't stop them. I let myself feel, because most of the time, I'm too afraid to feel. I hurt her, but I didn't want to. She's hurt me before as well.

I never know if she will hurt me again.

Whether it's her fault or not, that doesn't change what it does to my heart.

It also doesn't change what I just did to hers. I lost it, just like she does. "Do you ever feel like you're destined for something no matter how hard you try not to be?"

Ryder wraps his other arm around me. He's a whole head taller than I am, and his arms have moved up around my shoulders. I feel his lips press to the top of my head. "More than you know."

There once was a girl named Destiny. She was the fastest runner in the world.

No matter how hard she tried, she couldn't outrun who she was. Then she met a boy. He said his name was also Destiny, and for the first time in her life, she didn't feel like she was running alone.

Chapter Twenty-Two

Ryder

I heard everything Virginia and her mom said.

I don't know what the hell most of it meant. I heard stuff like, *how do I know you're you,* and *DID*, whatever that is. The only thing I do know is that it hurt Virginia, and I want to be the one who makes it better for her.

We sit on the bed and I almost tell her how strange this is again. I've never held a girl if she wasn't just a friend, or if I wasn't making out with her at the time, but I'm not sure how well that will go over. I've already told her more than once this situation is weird, and I'm not sure I want to keep drawing attention to that fact. I don't want her to realize it and make it go away.

After a while, her body language changes. She isn't holding me back, and then she's pulling away altogether.

"My dad will be home soon. I should take you home."

"Go with me," I nudge her. "I know you have a plan and this isn't part of it, but let's just go have fun tonight. My friends are going to a party on this private stretch of beach. Come with me. Get your mind off things, or whatever. You can even help me with my homework first." When she smiles, I wink at her.

"Yeah...sure...okay." Virginia calls her dad and tells him she's hanging out with her friends Jamie and Hailey tonight. I get a tightness in my chest, wondering if it's because of who I am that she's lying or if she would say the same thing if I went to her school.

When we get to my house, I run in and grab my backpack. We could stay here. We totally should stay here, but I don't tell her that. My house reminds me of all the ways we're different.

We park by our spot and do my homework in her car. Then we go into town and grab chicken nuggets and fries, sharing the meal in her car.

I give her directions to the spot where the party is. When we pull up, she pauses before getting out. Fear rushes through me as though someone injected it into my veins. "We won't get caught. We come here all the time. The cops don't bother with it." We're close enough that I can nudge her arm again. "If anything happens, I'll take care of you."

This gets her attention. Virginia turns my way and hits the interior light. "I can take care of myself."

"I know." Boss lady is an independent woman.

The words seem to surprise her, but she nods and says, "Thank you. For not asking, and for saying that. I..." Without continuing, she gets out of the car. I do the same and follow her to the back, where she opens the trunk. It's dark out, but there's a streetlight not too far away, showing me what she holds in her hand. "I got this for you the other day. Just in case."

A hoodie. A way better hoodie than I would have bought.

And she got it for me.

My chest starts to expand; okay maybe it's not, but it feels like…like it's growing and I can't fucking stop it. Things are moving around inside—shifting and making space. For her.

What are you doing to me? I want to ask her but I don't have the balls to do it. Instead, I kiss her. Like I always do, I have to tilt her head up because she's so much smaller than me. Our lips fit together, move together, and I sort of want to live here—in this moment, kissing Virginia.

She's the one who pulls away first. I pull the black hoodie on and zip it. The thing fits perfectly. "Let's go." I nod toward the water. It's a little hike to get there, which is probably why the cops don't bother.

We use our phones for flashlights as we make our way down the hidden embankment. There's a light in the distance, music playing and people yelling.

"Are you sure we won't get caught?" There's a slight hitch in her voice.

"I'll make sure you're okay. I promise."

It doesn't take long for us to make it to the party. There's got to be at least a hundred people here—college and high school students. I doubt there's anyone from Cliffton, except for Virginia.

Opening and closing my hand, I wonder if I should take hers. It's not something I've ever really thought about before and I don't want to do the wrong thing. Before I get the chance, I see Shane, Drea, Tanner and Cody sitting around a mini fire. Shane sees me first and nods his head. Tanner stands and then Cody and Shane do the same.

Drea is the last, her eyes sort of squinting as she takes us in.

"What's up?" I bump knuckles with all of them, except Drea, who doesn't offer hers.

"This is Virginia. Virginia, this is Shane, and Drea. The two who are attached to each other are Tanner and Cody."

I don't expect it to be Cody who holds his hand out and shakes hers first. "Hey."

"Hi," Virginia replies, and then Tanner and Shane tell her hello and shake her hand. When she gets to Drea, her hand isn't out.

"Gotta go. Darren just got here." She jogs off without another word. Darren's around a lot. I guess him and Drea are hooking up again.

They'd saved me a chair but I give that one to Virginia and take Drea's until she comes back. Tanner opens a small cooler. I try and shake my head at him but he doesn't notice and offers her a beer.

"No, thanks."

He looks at me next and I shake my head. I wonder what she sees when she looks at my friends. Shane is the most clean-cut-looking one of us. He has a piercing in his lip but that's it. His hair's black and shorter than mine. He almost looks like someone Virginia would know.

Tanner has his Mohawk, both his ears are pierced and he wears a lot of bracelets on his wrists. Cody's hair is obviously bleached, but darker underneath. It's messy as hell. He has at least one hand on Tanner all the time, almost like he needs him. He has drawings on his hands like tattoos. There's a flower covering the top of one and a random design on the other. They match some of the artwork he does around town.

We're a fucked up group.

What the hell was I thinking bringing her here?

"So...how much is he paying you to hang out with him?" Shane asks her. The second the words leave his mouth, his face pales as if he realizes how it sounds.

"What the fuck, man?" I make it halfway to my feet before Virginia is touching my hand and Shane is speaking.

"I didn't mean for it to sound like you're a hooker! I just wanted to give him shit, like he couldn't get a girl like you to hang out with him unless you're getting something out of it." He holds up his hands. "That was a bag on him. Not you, I swear."

Virginia is the first one to start laughing, followed by Shane. I collapse back into my seat, grateful that I don't have to kick my best friend's ass. It breaks the tension, and soon all of us are laughing. My friends start going off into other conversations. Once in a while, they ask Virginia something and she answers. The three of them are talking about something that happened at school when I look over and see her watching Tanner and Cody.

I get an uncomfortable feeling in my muscles. That's the one thing for me; I'll never have anything to do with someone who doesn't accept my friends. "You're staring," I whisper, surprised at the venom in my voice. I didn't want this from her. It'll mess everything up.

When she's speaks next, there's no anger. Its almost sounds like longing. "How long have they been together?"

"Like four years, or something."

"Cody...I think that's his name." She's looking at them but talking to me, quiet enough that no one else can hear her. "It's almost like he's afraid if he lets Tanner go, he'll disappear. Like he always wants to be touching him."

The words are familiar. They settle into my brain, as if to say, *isn't it obvious?* I thought the same thing about her earlier—I always want to touch her, and just today, I knew I had my hands on her to know she was really there.

Reaching over, I thread my fingers with Virginia's.

Chapter Twenty-Three

Virginia

Ryder's friends are different than I expected. I mean, they look how I thought they would and they talk how I thought they would. They drink and smoke, which I also expected. What I didn't count on was how kind they are to me. I'm not sure why I assumed they would be anything other than that. I guess it says something about me, and the kind of person I am.

It's not a mistake I plan to make again. It doesn't take a genius to figure out that they probably wouldn't be hanging out with me if I wasn't here with Ryder, but I am. Because they care for him, they try to get to know me, which I think is pretty cool of them.

Well, all of them except for Drea. She hasn't spoken a word to me all night. Another thing, it doesn't take a genius to see the reason why.

She's in love with Ryder. She hasn't taken her eyes off of him more than a few seconds all night, despite the fact that I've seen her kissing another guy and sitting on his lap. Most of the time, she only stops looking at Ryder to stare me down.

There's a part of me who wants to tell her that *he's mine,* but then I remind myself he's not really. They're close. They've been for a long time. They spend time together every day, so he's hers, too, even if it's not in the way she wants. Anyway, getting into a long-term relationship isn't part of my plan, and I'm sure it won't be long before Ryder gets bored with me.

But he is holding my hand. He's been doing it for over two hours now.

And I like it. I've liked it just as long as he's been doing it.

"Ry, think fast," Shane says to him as he tosses a beer Ryder's way. Our hands separate so he can reach out and catch it.

Ryder glances at me. "Nah, I'm good."

"You can," I whisper, silently glad he said no.

"It's cool."

"Who are *you*?" A deep voice says from beside me. I look up to see the guy Drea was with. He's eyeing me up and down.

"What the fuck, man? Don't talk to her like that." Ryder starts to stand but then Drea speaks.

"She's Ryder's girlfriend."

My heart nearly falls to my feet. *Oh God, he's going to assume I think he's my boyfriend.* "No, I'm not." The last thing I want is for him to believe I'm going to start pushing him; that just because we've kissed, I suddenly think we're serious. "Lulu. I'm Lulu."

"I thought your name was Virginia?" Shane asks.

"It is." My body starts to overheat, and not in the good way either. "Virginia's my first name and Lulu is my middle. I usually go by Lulu, but Ryder calls me Virginia. I hate my first name." *Shut up! Why am I still talking?*

My eyes dart toward Ryder, hoping he'll save me, but he's

looking toward the ground. His elbows rest on his knees as they bounce up and down.

"I gotta take a piss. I'll be right back." Ryder walks away, leaving me alone for the first time tonight. The instinct to ask him to wait teases my tongue, but I hold it back for two reasons. First, he's going to the bathroom. I don't need to be there for that. Second, I'm pretty sure I can be alone for a few minutes.

A shadow crosses in front of me and then Drea takes his seat. "I get it."

"Umm, get what?" I glance around, hoping Shane, Tanner or Cody will speak up; I don't want to be in a conversation with her alone. But the three of them are playfully arguing about something in their own world, and the guy she was kissing has left.

She lowers her voice, spite lighting her words. "Ryder. The attraction. It's the eyes that draw you in. Plus the fact that he's so obviously untamable, which of course makes us want to try. That's not the thing that keeps you around, though, is it? He kisses you like you're the only person in the world that matters."

Yeah...yeah he does. The words from her lips make my stomach turn.

"And we both know that's not the only thing he does well."

It's like a slap in the face. I don't know why it surprises me so much that they've been together. Drea is gorgeous. Her skin is just a few shades lighter than Jamie's, as though maybe only one of her parents is African American. Her eyelashes are super long, making her eyes stand out. She has a piercing between her lips and her nose. She could be a model.

She's one of Ryder's closest friends.

They've slept together.

She fits with him much more than I ever will.

I shouldn't want to fit with him.

She is in love with him.

"You're right about that. Kissing isn't the only thing he does well." What. The. Heck. Did I just say? She eases away from me as though she didn't expect the words. That makes two of us, but I also don't want her to think she can chase me off...even though we both know I don't belong here anyway.

"Whatever." The camp chair falls backward when Drea stands, and then she walks away. As soon as she's out of sight, I push to my feet as well. I have to get out of here. Have to.

I don't make it ten feet before I hear Ryder. "Where are you going?" He steps up beside me.

"Home. I need to go home. I can give you a ride, but I'm sure you'd rather go with your friends."

"Way to push it off on me. I'm sure *you'd* rather I go with my friends."

"What is that supposed to mean?" I don't stop walking.

"Fuck," he mumbles. "Nothing." He doesn't stop going, either.

"What are you doing?" *Go with me...*

"Walking you to your car. I'm not a complete asshole."

I bite my tongue to keep from speaking the whole walk to my car. It takes a few minutes to get there, and we're alone when we do. I'm not even sure what I'm going to say when I open my mouth. I just let words fall out. "You've had sex with Drea?"

Courtesy of the light above the car, I see him flinch, but recover quickly. "Yeah, why does it matter? That's in the past."

It shouldn't matter, and I know that, but somehow it does.

"It's not a big deal, Virginia. It's not like we're in a relationship or anything. We're friends. We trust each other. We like to have a good time. It's nothing."

Maybe to him it's nothing, but it is to her. *It is to me as well.* I'm not comfortable knowing he's got a hot friend-with-benefits on the side.

"What I can't figure out is why you care. You're the one who said I wasn't your boyfriend." He crosses his arms and almost sounds...hurt? But that doesn't make sense.

"What are you talking about? You made it clear you don't really want a girlfriend."

"And you said the same thing about having a boyfriend!"

"And it's not like you *asked* me to be your girlfriend or anything."

Ryder's head snaps up at that, his eyes meeting mine. His demeanor changes, the anger slipping out of his stance. I can't tell what it's replaced by, but it's totally different.

"Would it really matter if I did?"

Yes. Yes, it would matter. But would it really? I have a plan I have to stick to, and Ryder isn't in it. He's wild and reckless and I would bore him. I'm supposed to want to bore a boy like him. Instead of saying any of that, I take the easy way out. "She's in love with you... Drea...she loves you." Only it turns out the words aren't as easy as I thought they would be. They make my chest ache so bad I wish I could double over and hold myself. Curl into a ball and cry. I turn away from him.

"Hey..." Ryder steps closer, his hands on my shoulders. "Did she say something to you? That's just how Drea is. She's tough, and she probably feels defensive because she's really the only girl who hangs around us. I know…I know this probably makes me an asshole—I know you wouldn't do something like this or want to be with a guy who does—but when I've been with her, it's not because we're in love with each other. It's just…familiar, I guess. It's just a way to have fun. Shit, that sounds so fucked up." The sincerity in his words runs deep. Ryder believes what he's saying, but she's in love with him. And when he finds that out, it could change everything.

Drea is his friend. She's familiar. She's fun. Why wouldn't he want that?

Slowly, I turn to face him. "She's in love with you. I saw it all night. She looks at you the way Cody looks at Tanner. The way Tanner looks at Cody." My eyes sting. *Oh God.* I hear it, the whisper that starts deep inside me, getting louder and louder. The one that says *the way you want Ryder to look at you.*

He's going to ruin everything. *I'm* going to ruin everything. He's a distraction I don't need…but one I want. He makes me want to change my plan. "I have to go."

Ryder doesn't try to stop me as I get into my car and drive away.

Chapter Twenty-Four

Ryder

I don't move from where she left until I can't see the lights from her car anymore. Even when there's nothing but darkness on the road, I stay still. What just happened?

All I wanted was to make this night good for her. I wanted to be with her. I brought her to meet my friends and I held her hand and I thought of her as my girlfriend, yet she bailed on me because I'm friends with Drea? Because of something that's happened between us that I can't take back?

She's the one who said she didn't want to be with me.

Suddenly, I can't stop my legs from moving. Back and forth, I pace the area where she'd been parked. Where she gave me a hoodie and I told her I would make sure she's okay.

She's Ryder's girlfriend...

No, I'm not...

Dude, I've been so stupid. What the hell was I thinking spending time with her and thinking it could actually mean something? That, what? I'd be like one of the guys at her school, and walk down the street holding her hand? That she would actually have a reason to want me as her boyfriend?

But I wanted it. I can't believe I wanted it, and that makes me more pissed at myself than anything.

My foot connects with something. Looking down, I see a glass bottle rolling away. Bending over, I pick it up, and throw it as hard as I can. I watch the glass shatter as it hits the light pole and wonder how some girl I just met has the power to make my insides feel like they're doing that—like they're shattering.

It takes me less than half the time it took with her to reach the party again. I go straight for one of the kegs, fill a cup and drain the whole thing. I fill another and I'm halfway through it when there's a familiar hand on my arm.

"Let it go, man. I don't want to talk about it."

Shane cocks his head slightly. "You really like her."

My answer is to empty my second cup before filling another. Downing beer that quickly makes it straight to my head. I'm halfway through my third cup when I start to get the spins.

"Ryder," Shane says, but I walk away from him. Fire dances in front of my eyes so I make a turn to keep from falling into it.

Tanner and Cody watch me. Tanner stands, but then Cody grabs his wrist and keeps him there.

"Ryder Blackstock, you're wasted." This girl who goes to my school wraps her arms around my shoulders. We're facing each other and I smile at her.

"I am." But then I step backward and her hands unlatch and fall to her sides. Without another word, I walk away, walk closer to the hill that leads up to the parking. I keep going until it's darker, until the party feels a million miles away, even though I can still see it, before I collapse into the sand.

Who the hell am I?

I've always known who I am. Always. And I've always been okay with that. Yet one rich girl shows me a little attention and I, what? Think I can be someone else? Think the world works in a way where it doesn't matter that my dad's a criminal and I'm a thief when she'll really be somebody one day?

I know better than that.

"Hey."

I put my hands behind my head as I lie in the sand, and close my eyes. "What did you say to her, Dre?"

"Does it matter?" She sits so close to me I feel her side touch mine. "You were afraid to even be yourself around her, Ry. Would she have gotten mad at you if you drank a beer in front of her?"

"This is because I didn't have a beer? Maybe I just didn't want one." My head gets dizzy when I jerk into a sitting position.

"Obviously you didn't want a drink, seeing as how you had a shitload the moment she left."

"Funny." There's never been a time in my life that I've been mad at Drea. I've been upset if she let some guy treat her like crap, or when she's down on herself. This is different, though. Anger starts overpowering my buzz. No, it's not just anger, either. Mixing through all that red, hot heat inside me is something else. Pain.

She betrayed me. There's nothing I wouldn't do for Drea, and she tried to take away something that made me feel good for the first time in a long time, maybe the first time in forever. She saw me holding Virginia's hand. She had to know Virginia means something to me.

And she does. She means a lot, and I'm not sure what to do

141

with that. "What the fuck is wrong with me?" My body rocks back and forth, back and forth. I lock my hands together behind my head, elbows forward, and close my eyes.

"Oh my God." Drea's voice is hardly over a whisper. She pushes away from me. Not too far, but putting space there. "You're in love with her."

"No." I shake my head, because I'm not. I can't be. It's not like we even really know that much about each other. I just know how she makes me feel. That she's implanted herself inside me, and I like her there. "I like her, though. A lot. Dude, I sound like an idiot. It's so whacked hearing myself say that." But it's true. I like Virginia. I've never let myself do that before.

Shane's my best friend, but I couldn't have said that to him. Probably couldn't with Tanner or Cody, either. Dre and I have always been close like that, which is why I already feel the anger seeping out of my bones.

"She thinks you're in love with me."

It's as though someone hit a mute button and there's no sound except the waves in the distance. Drea stares off into the dark. She doesn't speak. Doesn't move. And I know, *know*, that Virginia was right.

"Dre?" She looks at me for a second, her eyes glassy, and then puts a hand to her mouth.

Holy shit. How can she be in love with me? How could I not know it? Maybe to some people that would be a stupid question, but we've always been friends. It's not like I'm the only guy she's ever kissed at a party or messed around with just to have a good time, the same way she's not the only girl I've done that with. It's just sort of the way things are.

I grab her and pull her to me. She comes easily, burying her face in my neck as she cries. Drea doesn't cry. She doesn't let anyone or anything have that effect on her, yet she's crying in my arms.

Her hands fist the hoodie Virginia gave me. Each time her body shakes, it vibrates through me. It makes my chest feel like it's opened up; parts of me falling out into the sand.

I never wanted to hurt her. Ever.

There is no buzz left inside me as I hold her. When her tears finally stop, she pulls away.

"I'm sorry. I swear I didn't know."

She wipes her eyes with the back of her hand. "Then you're blind. And you're the only one."

What? I glance toward the party where our friends are.

"I didn't tell them, but I'm pretty sure they can see it."

I rub my chest as though that will make the ache go away. "There's someone better for you out there than me."

"What? A Virginia for me, too?"

Nudging her, I say, "I figured he'd be a guy."

Pretending things are okay doesn't feel right, though. Drea wraps her arms around herself.

I can't believe this is happening. "You know it kills me to hurt you. I never wanted that. I love you, Drea. You're one of my best friends. I don't know what I'd do without you."

"I know." She whispers.

My four friends know everything about me and they accept the whole package. They know who my dad is and what I've done. They love me regardless, and that means something to me.

"I'm sorry I messed things up with your girl."

I shake my head. "It's not your fault."

"You're totally falling for her."

Shrugging is the only reply I can manage. We both know I am.

"You should go see her. Throw rocks at her window and climb up a tree by her room. Girl's like her like stuff like that, right?"

A small laugh falls out of my mouth. "Not Virginia. She's too practical for that."

"Go see her, Ryder."

"Nah. It never would have worked anyway. And I'm not going to ditch you."

"You're not. Plus...I think it might be easier not to be around you right now."

I tense up.

"Not forever. Just tonight...or something."

I've already hurt her enough. Whatever she wants I'll do to make this easier on her. Pulling her closer to me, I press my lips to her forehead.

"Go." She pushes me gently, so I do.

I head straight to Shane first. I tell him where Drea is and to go and be with her. He nods, already heading that way when I call his name. "Can I have your keys? I need Tanner to take me somewhere real quick, and then he can come back."

Without a second thought, he tosses them my way. Tanner's been drinking but Cody's sober, so it's him who gets behind the wheel.

My leg is actually bouncing up and down, I'm so nervous. This is a huge mistake. It'll probably backfire on me, but I can't leave things the way they are. Not with her.

Chapter Twenty-Five

Virginia

It's seven a.m. when I finally admit that I'm not going to get any sleep and get out of bed. My night was spent tossing and turning. Every time my eyes finally closed, I dreamt about Mom not being Mom or her being sad, or Ryder realizing that Drea loves him and it opening his eyes to how he feels about her.

My nightmares would jerk me out of sleep, and I'd be partially grateful for the reprieve from my subconscious, only to actively think about everything while awake.

It doesn't make for the best night's sleep.

When I make it to the bottom of the stairs, the first thing I see is Dad with a cup of coffee, sitting at the dining room table. The table. I really don't know if I can do this today.

Turning, I plan to sneak back upstairs when I hear, "I see you, Lulu. Get yourself a cup of coffee and join me."

Dad's the most understanding person I know. He doesn't ask for much. The least I can do is listen.

I do as he said before sitting at the table with a hot mug of coffee in hand. "I didn't mean to hurt her." And I didn't. But it doesn't change anything—not how I feel, or the brokenness of my heart, or the fact that I'm scared to death to fall victim to her curse.

"I know you didn't, kiddo, but you still did."

"I—"

Dad holds up his hand to tell me to wait. "And I know she's hurt you. You're not her, Lulu. I know that's what you're scared of, but I'm telling you, you're not."

How can he possibly know that? He didn't know everything about her when they fell in love. Mom didn't always suffer with her disease. She told me stories. I know all about her adventures when she was a teenager. How she suddenly started to feel different when on the streets. I know she gradually began losing time, going places she didn't remember going. Wanting things she'd never wanted.

Just like I wanted to go with her to LA that night because it sounded fun.

The same way I spontaneously climbed onto a dock that I knew could get me killed.

He didn't know that I've had urges and desires—little pulls to do things that aren't me, so I throw myself into school or homework instead.

Even the way I said hurtful things to her yesterday. That's something Samantha would have done.

Perfect, Fear, Guilt, Lonely, Destiny. Maybe I'm already more people than just Lulu.

Or maybe I'll get so wrapped up in school that I'll cut myself off from my friends and become a loner. Get depressed.

I could even lose myself in Ryder and rebel against the person I'm trying so hard to be, and go too far off the other end.

My finger starts to twitch and I watch it, lost in the uncontrollable movement. There are so many things I can be, so many ways I can go wrong. How do I know what's right? How do I keep myself level?

"How do you know?" For once, I don't have an answer. I want so badly for Dad to have one.

He looks sad as he pushes out of the chair and walks over to me, kneels next to my chair. "Life is messy, kiddo. I guess none of us ever know what will happen. But your situation is different than Mom's. You don't live the same life she did. You don't live in the same world. And," Dad shrugs, "you're strong. So strong. I wish you saw that."

I want to be. More than anything, I want that.

"Your mother woke up one day, and your grandma was gone. A few years later, she found out her mom had passed. Don't be afraid to live. And hold onto the people you love. Those are the two most important things I can tell you."

Dad kisses my forehead. "And you're going to have to talk to her. Soon." He pushes to his feet and glances at his watch. "I have to run into the city. I forgot something at the office. Do you want to tag along? We can have lunch afterward or something."

Before he finishes getting the words out, I'm already shaking my head. My mind is so stuffed with—*life* that I just need to be alone right now.

"Okay. I'll be back in a few hours."

"I'll walk you out. I left my phone in my car last night." Which isn't something I would typically care about. It's not as though I talk on it much. I don't want to think about the reason I want it.

Dad's car is parked next to mine in the driveway. He goes to the driver side as I walk around the far side to my car. Something catches my eye and I glace to the side of the house. My heart drops to my stomach as I see Ryder sitting around the corner with his hood over his head, his knees up and his arms on top of them. His head's on his arms and he's sleeping.

Outside.

In the cold.

It can get into the lower fifties or cooler, at night in September.

"Lulu?"

"Yeah?" I whip around to face Dad again.

"Bye. Are you sure you're okay? There's still time if you want to go with me."

"No! I mean," I lower my voice. "No. It's fine." Ryder is *sleeping* outside my house right now.

"Okay." Dad gets in the car, then starts it and rolls down the window. "Aren't you going to get your phone?"

Oh yeah. Duh. "Yep." I unlock my car, the whole time hoping Dad doesn't see Ryder on the side of the house. So many questions are going through my head. What's he doing here? How long has he been outside? How do I feel about that?

The second Dad's car pulls away, I turn to Ryder. He's woken up now, but still sits in the same spot as if he's afraid to move.

"This isn't as screwed up as it looks," he finally says.

"Ryder!" I walk toward him. "It's cold. What are you doing here?" I grab his hand and he lets me help him up. It doesn't matter that he's possibly in love with another girl right now, or that we got in a fight. He's huddled up against my house on a cold, Sunday morning, and I need to warm him up. "Come on, let's go inside."

His hands are shaking; other than that, he doesn't move. "Wait. You were right about Drea. I didn't know. If I had...I'm not the kind of guy who would do something like that and know he's hurting someone. I would never want to hurt her."

Oh. And I guess I knew that. If not, I wouldn't have hung out with him. There's a gentle soul inside there. He's showed it to me many times. As much as I like that about him, he still makes my body ache in ways I didn't know were possible. He really didn't know, but now he does. That has to mean something to him.

"She's one of my best friends." Ryder shoves his hands into his pants pockets and looks away from me.

So he's come here to let me down, face to face. Crossing my arms, I rock slightly back and forth. It's something to pass the time. I'm not really a rocker, but I don't know what else to do. It's not like I didn't know this would happen. It's not like it isn't for the best.

"Thanks... You really might have saved my life that night." Or at least my sanity. "You're..." Oh God. I'm going to cry. I've never cried this much in my life. My whole body feels out of whack. I wanted to change my plan with Ryder. I wanted to be his girlfriend. I wanted to believe all my worries are impossible when I'm with him.

"I should go back in."

"Virginia."

Ryder's voice makes me stop in my tracks. It whispers against my skin even though he's too far away to touch me. It burrows its way inside me as though I opened myself up to him. It's familiar, yet not. It's needy. It speaks to me as though I've

149

been deaf my whole life, and this is the first time I've heard words.

"It's not Drea for me."

It takes an eternity for me to face him. When I do, Ryder's not looking at me. His hands are still in his pockets and his eyes still somewhere else.

"I…" he shrugs. "It's you."

Chapter Twenty-Six

Ryder

It's crazy how the words don't even bother me. I expected to feel like an idiot saying them. Maybe that's exactly how I sound, but her knowing what's going on inside me is more important. There's never really been anyone who makes me feel so much before, and I don't want to hold it in. I still remember how it felt when Luke told me about all his colleges, when I knew he was leaving. I didn't say a word, just held it in and got over it. It was the same loneliness when Virginia walked away last night, and now, I don't want to just get over it.

She stares at me, wide-eyed.

"It's cool if you don't feel the same. I get it. But I needed to say it, so I did."

My bones feel brittle, the cold having set in them all night, which might put me into psycho territory—the fact that I chilled outside her house all night. This is where I should walk away. Virginia hasn't moved from her spot a few feet away from me. She's probably trying to figure out what the hell is happening here, which makes two of us. I'm an alien in my own skin right now, but I don't try and force the foreign body out.

Finally, after what feels like ten lifetimes, she whispers, "It's you for me, too…but I'm scared."

That's all it takes for me to move toward her. I pull her against me, her head tucks under my chin and her arms wrap around my waist. She feels so good—warm and soft and comfortable.

I won't tell her there's no reason to be afraid, because we both know there is. She doesn't even know who I am, and yet she has to sense it. We're so different. She wants things I've never considered wanting, and has things I'll probably never be able to have.

I've done things she would have every right to hate me for. There's no way it will work and no way it will last, but this right here? Holding her? It's almost enough to make me forget the rest of it.

I shiver and then she does. For some reason, it makes me smile. I wonder if what I'm feeling seeped into her, and I sort of like the thought of that. Still, I don't want her to be cold. "It's freezing balls out here. You should go in. We can talk later."

Virginia leans back. "You have such a way with words."

I shrug because I can't help who I am.

"Come in with me."

"Your dad…"

"We have a few hours."

Works for me.

I take her hand and we go inside. Her house looks the same, but also as though it's this uncharted territory. This is the first time I'm in her house when she knows how I feel about her. That

I'm not just here because she's hot, and I want to make out with her.

Virginia closes the door to her room behind us.

"A bed. I never thought I would see one of these again," I tease as I kick out of my shoes and climb in. It's the first time I've been in her room where it's not perfectly made. I pull the covers over myself and take her in for the first time. Her hair is in a messy ponytail. She's never worn one of those before, and she has on matching, flannel pajamas. "Even have to be coordinated to go to sleep, huh?"

"Shut up," she tells me, lingering beside her bed.

"Lay down, Virginia. I'm just trying to get warm."

She pauses a second and then gets under the blankets with me. "What do you think happens when you stay outside all night?"

There's a slight awkwardness between us. We're both on our backs, looking at the ceiling, our sides hardly touching. I want to bridge the distance. "I didn't plan to. Cody and Tanner dropped me off. I tried throwing pebbles at your window, but that shit doesn't work. How in the hell is that supposed to wake someone up? I tried your phone, but you didn't answer. Then I sat down for a second to figure out what to do and…I fell asleep."

"What? That's crazy. How do you just fall asleep quickly like that?"

"I've slept in worse places. Dad used to always have people around so I'm good with passing out no matter how loud it is or how cold I might be." It's those words that open the door for tension to fill the room again. Just another way we're different.

I let the silence stretch on because I can tell there's something she wants to say. Finally, she lets the question out. "Why me?

We don't have the same idea of what's fun. I do homework to clear my head, and I'm obsessed with college. I don't party, and I can be bitchy and judgmental. Drea's fun. She's wild, strong, beautiful, and—"

"You're strong and beautiful."

She chuckles softly and shakes her head.

"It's just a different kind of strength. You are who you are, and you don't care what people think. You don't care that you're sober at a party where everyone is drinking. You don't give a shit if you're the girl who leaves to do her homework, because it's important to you."

"Is it still strength if the reason behind it is fear?" She sounds like she's drifting away, her voice getting softer and softer. I need to reel her back in, keep her close, so I roll to my side, lean my head into my hand and let my elbow prop me up. With my other hand, I brush her cheek with my thumb.

"I don't know. You're the smart one. Regardless, I know you're strong." Because I know she's dealing with more than I've seen; I just don't have a clear picture of what it is.

"We're still different, though, so why me?"

Words get trapped in my throat. I can tell her it's because of what I said—she's beautiful and strong. I can tell her it's because sometimes the loneliness in her eyes mirrors mine, only I didn't know it was there before her. Maybe it's to prove I won't screw up with a girl like her the way Luke thinks I will. There are a million possibilities, not all of them good. The only thing that manages to come out is, "Because the weight isn't as heavy when I'm with you."

Her breath hitches. I let my fingers gently glide against her neck, her throat. When she speaks, I feel the words vibrate through my fingertips. It's a crazy-wild feeling, and I want it to keep going, want to touch all her words.

"The weight of what?" she asks.

I don't know... I shrug. "Of everything."

But it's not my words that settle into my chest. It's hers. Virginia shakes her head and answers her own question. "Of destiny."

It's in this moment that I realize I'm not sure if the life I've always seen for myself is the one I want. Maybe it is and maybe it isn't. I've always just accepted it, accepted my fate, my destiny. Dad always told me I was good, and I needed that. Craved to be good at something. Dad never asked, he just assumed.

Luke tells me it's not what I want, tells me I'm stupid for the things I've done. He never asks, either.

But is it what I want?

I count that as another thing I don't know. There's one thing I know for sure, though. "Virginia?"

"Yeah." She rolls her head to the side slightly so we're making eye contact.

"Just so we're clear this time, I want you to be my girlfriend."

Her smile is so big I think it could make the whole world happy. "Yes."

Chapter Twenty-Seven

Virginia

The next couple of weeks are a mixture of strange and wonderful—wonderfully strange, I guess. In some ways, I've become the girl I never thought I would be. The one who hangs out with her boyfriend every day and thinks about him when he's not there and wonders how on Earth they'll ever make this work.

The kicker is, the world hasn't come crashing in yet. Homework is still the first thing I do after school; it's just now I'm doing it with Ryder. We managed to get the principal to take our proposal to the school board about the showers. I'm making great progress in FBLA.

So, in other words, I'm still me.

That doesn't mean I'm the girl who will skip school for no reason, or the one who will be dancing on tabletops at a party. Ryder and responsibility seem to be two things I can handle together, so maybe I can be the girl who doesn't lose her head to a boyfriend. Who can balance the two because they're the things I want more than anything else.

That doesn't mean I'm not scared out of my mind, though. It doesn't mean that when the bell rings after English and I get asked to stay after, that my heart isn't running a marathon.

"How are things going with you, Lulu?"

Sometimes it's so weird when a teacher asks a normal question like that. It's as though they think you're friends or something. I mean, it's not that I dislike my teachers. I respect what they do, but the divide is always there, and when someone tries to cross it, things get out of whack. "Fine."

"I'm excited about your mom's new book. Have you read it?"

Especially when they're a fan of your mom's. Especially when they think that will bring you closer when all it does it make you want to crawl out of your own skin.

I often wonder if Mom sacrificed herself for what she does. Maybe to others, that doesn't make sense, but she puts so much of herself into the books she writes. She'll stay locked in her office for days or randomly disrupt my schooling to try and get me to go on a work trip with her, so that other people can lose themselves in the world of her characters. Has she lost herself to them, as well? Is that what happened to Annette Klinger, Virginia Woolf, and Sylvia Plath? Do they give so much of themselves to people who aren't real that they lose who they are? Their grip on what reality is or is not?

"No, I haven't."

Mrs. Young frowns but then tries to cover it. It's almost as though she's seeing more than I'm saying. As if I'm wearing my fear, when I've never done that before. "I better get to class."

"Wait." She reaches into her desk and pulls out a manila envelope. "I know you weren't sure if you're interested, but I got the entry packet for you. You're the most skilled writer I've had the pleasure of teaching, Lulu."

"I'm going into business."

"You're still moving on to higher education, and any and all accolades you get can only help you."

Why?, I want to ask her. *Why are you pushing this?*

"You should be proud of your talent. I can only imagine how happy it must make your mother."

Because I'm automatically destined to be like she is. Only, I won't accept that. "I'm not interested."

"Take it anyway. You never know."

So I do. It's almost as if the package burns my hand as I carry it, before it opens a wound and lets my curiosity free. I wonder what kind of story they want.

"Mommy, look! I wrote a story. Daddy helped me type it."

Mom hasn't even read it, yet her eyes are already filled with glassy excitement. "You did, Virginia? Let me see it. I want to read it."

I dance around the room as her eyes scan my adventure about the girl who writes fantastical stories that transport her to whatever world she creates. Whatever she writes comes true. My blood rushes when I think of fighting dragons, and winning the hand of the prince. There are so many journeys I want to take.

"Come here, Virginia. Give me a hug."

I run into Mom's arms and hold her.

"This is so good. One day you'll write stories even better than mine."

Dad walks into the room and grins. "Like mother, like daughter."

Not going to happen.

I shove the envelope into my backpack and go about my day. I don't care about the papers in my bag, about fantasy worlds

and living out other people's lives. I have my own real life to
worry about.

Chapter Twenty-Eight

Ryder

"I'm thinking about getting a job." Twisting the knob, I turn up the heater in Virginia's car.

"What about school?" She sounds scandalized.

"What about it? I'm not dropping out or anything." It's a struggle, but I manage not to laugh at her. She's irritated, I can tell, though she won't tell me why. Her dad's home today, so we can't go to her house. It's stupid of me not to invite her to mine, but letting her see the inside of my house is almost letting her see the real me. Messy and dirty. When we're at her place, I can pretend.

"My dad is big on not working while I'm in school. I know a lot of people do it, and that's great, but now's the time to be focusing on our academics."

This time, I can't help but chuckle. She sounds like I imagine her mom and dad sound when they tell her that.

"Ugh. Whatever."

Yep, she's definitely pissy. "We need to go somewhere and

do your homework, STAT. We're reaching dangerous levels here."

Her body tenses up slightly.

"Hey. I'm kidding. What's wrong?" I reach over and set my hand on her leg.

"Nothing. Why do you want to get a job?"

Her words make my guts twist up. It's what she did in the beginning, like the second night we were at the water when she asked me questions instead of answering them. It's her way of keeping me out. "Because I feel like a piece of shit since either Shane has to take me to your school or you have to pick me up every day. Not that I'd be able to save to get a car anytime soon. By the time I got one…" She'll be off at Stanford. And no, it's not far, but I'm not delusional enough to think she's still going to want to be with me then.

"It doesn't matter." Virginia glances my way.

Maybe not to her, but it does to me. I grab one of the strings on my hoodie and wrap it around my finger.

"I wish we could go to my house." She drums her fingers on the steering wheel.

Me, too… But I get it. I'm not the guy she could bring home to dad.

"What about your place? I want to meet Luke, too. Does he hate me? He seemed like he hated me that one time I saw him outside."

"Nope. He hates me is more like it. Plus, he's not at home. You don't want to go to my house, it sucks. And you don't want to meet my brother, either." Which really means that I don't want her to meet him. Not for the same reasons she doesn't want her dad knowing me, though. Her dad will tell her I'm not good enough. I'm afraid Luke will make her see the same thing.

"Gee, thanks for telling me how I feel. Are we at that stage in the relationship where our thoughts aren't our own?"

Ouch. "That's not what I meant and you know it. And what's wrong with you? You're being stabby."

"Stabby?"

That makes the corners of her mouth pull up slightly. I hadn't even meant to use the word. It's something Drea says sometimes. My chest gets an ache, right in the center. It's been strained with my friends lately. It's weird with Dre, which makes it uncomfortable for all of us. "I got it from someone."

Virginia pulls up to a red light and looks my way. The green of her eyes is darker, sadder. I'm not sure if it's because she knows it's Drea or because of whatever has her in a bad mood.

"You miss them."

"They're still around."

"We don't have to hang out every day."

"Yeah, but I don't get to kiss them. You're more fun." I wait, hoping for a smile that doesn't come. There's a honk behind us and then she drives again.

After a minute of silence, I say, "I'm where I wanna be."

"Me, too…" She sounds sadder about that than she should be. "My English teacher… She's pushing me on this writing thing she wants me to do. It's a competition."

"You don't want to?" The words almost don't compute. Virginia equals school. I can't understand why she wouldn't want to do whatever they think she should.

"No."

"Why does she want you to?"

She shrugs. "Because of who my mom is…and because she thinks I'm good."

"Why don't you want to?"

It takes her a minute, but then she says, "The same reasons."

This time it's her who reaches towards me. Virginia threads her fingers through mine and it does something to me, makes me feel like there isn't anything I can't do. She's looking for me to ground her right now.

"I'll never push you with shit like that. If you want to tell me, I'm here. If you don't, I won't try and talk you into it." We all have our own shit, and we deal with it in our own way.

"It's not like you probably don't know… You heard her that day. One internet search is all it would take."

She's right about that. After that day she fought with her mom, I've always known something is up with them, known she somehow hurts Virginia. They tossed around a lot of crap. The letters DID stuck out. "I didn't look it up. I wanted to, but I didn't. Like I said, I won't push. I want to know, but only if you tell me, not because I think I deserve to know. Not because I went behind your back." Luke has always been in my business like that. He never wants to hear what I say, because he's already decided the answers before he speaks to me.

"Hey." I release her hand and wipe the one tear that escapes her eye. "Why are you crying?"

"Because you're better than you realize, Ryder Blackstock. It scares me as much as it sets me free."

She deserves to be free from whatever it is that's trapping her. And I want that, what she said, to be true. I want to be better than who I've always thought I am.

"Turn left at the next light. I know where we can go."

Chapter Twenty-Nine

Virginia

Ryder leads me to a diner, or a café, I guess. *Annie's Café*. I don't really know why we're here.

"Do they have good food here, or something?" Even if they do, Ryder doesn't typically want to go out, because he often doesn't have money. It bothers him, though I wish it didn't. Money doesn't matter to me. Not that I don't know I'm blessed to have it. I do, but it's not important to me that he doesn't have what I do.

"Come on. Let's go in." He nods toward the building. It has a big, red awning around half of it with windows all along the front.

He has his backpack up front with him, so he grabs it. I take mine out of the back, and then follow him as he walks. It's funny how you can tell a mood someone's in just by seeing them from behind. Their body language tells the story for them, and Ryder's is saying he's nervous.

He holds the door open for me, this boy with piercings in his lip, who likes to party and doesn't really care about school, though I'm not really sure how true the last part is. I think he cares; he just never had anyone who let him show it. He's stubborn. If you push, he pushes back so it's important to just let him be.

"Thanks."

"No problem—"

"Hey, Ryder!" A girl with red hair cuts him off. She looks like she's in her early twenties and she's gorgeous. "We don't see you here often."

The café is about three-quarters of the way full. There are servers busily moving around from table to table. It's loud but not too bad.

"Got an empty table for us; kind of out of the way? Virginia needs to do her homework." Virginia, not we.

It's the first time the girl notices me. Her nose wrinkles. Not in a mean way, but a shocked one. "Yeah, sure. One just emptied in the back corner. Let me clean it for you real quick. Your brother's around here somewhere. He's in a mood. Night waitress called in so he's going to have to stay."

Oh. Now, I get why he's nervous. Luke works here. I don't know why Ryder's strange about us meeting, but I know this is a big deal for him.

The waitress walks away as the door to the kitchen swings open. A man walks out of the same door and I know immediately who it is...Luke. He looks so similar to Ryder. They're both tall and built the same. They both walk like they carry the weight of the world, and their eyes try to hide who they are. I didn't realize it the first time I saw him. Part of me wants to be shy, but my instincts take over, instincts I hope are right as I shake the nerves out of my hand before threading my fingers through Ryder's.

Luke looks down at our hands, up into my eyes, and gives me

a small shake of his head.

"Virginia, this is my brother, Luke. Luke, this is my Virginia. I mean, Virginia. My…girlfriend."

It's as though Ryder took a stun gun to his brother. He doesn't move at first, in this obvious sort of trance, but then he snaps out of it and holds his hand out. I have to let go of Ryder's hand to shake it.

"Hey…um… it's nice to meet you."

"You, too," I reply.

"We're gonna go sit down. Meg's cleaning a table for Virginia to do her homework." Ryder latches onto my hand again and then heads toward the back of the restaurant, leaving Luke to watch us in shock. Meg is just finishing up. She smiles and asks if we want anything as we slide into the booth. Ryder glances at me. "Can you get Virginia a Diet Dr. Pepper? I'll just have water. Do you want anything to eat? We can get a menu."

Shaking my head is easier than replying. He knows my drink. Without me telling him, he knows my drink. It makes my insides turn to mush.

Meg leaves and Ryder scrolls through his phone as I pull work from my bag.

"You don't have to do that, you know." I don't look at him.

"Do what?"

I open my math book. "You're not proving your brother, Meg or anyone else right by not doing your homework. Maybe they expect it, maybe they don't, but they don't matter. Only you do." I shrug. "Only what you want."

He sets his phone on the table, spinning it as he watches it. It represents his mind. I imagine all the wheels turning in there, thinking about what I said. Or maybe not even my words, but how he feels. I won't pretend to get Ryder's relationship with his brother. What I do know is, if we were at my house, he would automatically be doing his work with me.

Maybe I'm delusional. Maybe I want to pretend that's the real Ryder, he's just kept him in hiding, when in reality, he pretends when he's with me.

When he peers up, his multi-colored eyes connecting with mine, I see mischief there. "But how will I get my reward if we're in public?"

"Oh my God. Shut up." I toss a napkin at him. Yes, the making out between assignments will pretty much be non-existent here. "Don't pretend that's why you do it." It better not be. Then I add, "I guess that means I'll have to double up on your reward next time." My face burns and I can't look at him.

"That's what I'm talking about." Ryder opens his bag and pulls out his binder and books. Meg brings our drinks and we each get started, doing our thing. About twenty minutes in, he whispers, "Hey."

"Yes?" I roll my pen between my fingers, still staring at my books.

"Thanks... For reeling me back in. For not expecting anything one way or another. Just letting me know it's okay to be me."

If I wasn't already there, it's those words that would make my heart take a header off the cliff, diving all the way in love with Ryder.

"It's not an act with you. You know who you are more than anyone I've met."

That's where he's wrong about me. "No, I don't. I just try harder to create the person I want to be."

I don't know if that's a good thing or bad, but it's real.

Meg keeps the water and Diet Dr. Pepper coming. Ryder and I move from subject to subject. He takes breaks to tease me from time to time. We laugh a lot, like we always do.

When we're finished with our work, I look at my phone. "I should go. Dad's making dinner tonight. Do you want me to take you home?"

He gets a sad, sort of smile on his face and shakes his head. "Nah. I'll chill here for a while. Maybe call Shane to come get me. I'll walk you out, though."

He waits as I pack my bag, and then reaches out to carry it for me. I feel like Hailey did that night I told her about Ryder—I practically saw the hearts and butterfly bubbles floating around her head.

Oh God. I'm *that* girl. I'm totally a romantic.

Since it's Ryder, I'm okay with that.

When we get to the car, he puts my bag in the back. I lean against the driver door and Ryder steps in closely. He touches my hair like he always does. Watches it slide through his fingers. And then he leans his forearms on my car, one on either side of my head, and drops his forehead to mine.

"I had this dream last night. I was sleeping in the dream, and then I woke up. I was in my room, but it wasn't in my house. It was a big house, like yours. My stuff was new, and my carpet was soft. I got dressed, and when I looked in the mirror, my piercings weren't there, but it was like they'd never been there. I went downstairs and Luke and I had dinner with our dad. He wore a suit and drank orange juice. After we ate, I went to pick you up in my car. We met Dre, Shane, Tan and Cody at school 'cause we all went to the same one. It was nice like your school."

I wish I could show him my heart so he could see it breaking for him, so he could know that the organ beating in my chest is his; but I'm scared to tell him.

"It's strange, because that's not me. We know it never will be, Virginia, and I've never wanted it to be. I like my piercings. I don't want a dad who wears a suit, and I'll probably always be kind of a dickhead. But it felt normal in the dream. It felt right for you."

I can't find words so I find his mouth instead. My hands hold the sides of his face and I slip my tongue into his mouth. I want to breathe him in. Memorize his taste on my tongue, and show him that who we are or who we think we should be doesn't matter. I want to make myself believe it as much as I need Ryder to see it, because as much as I want it to be true, I'm still who I am and he's still who he is. Not that I don't think those people are good for each other, but because I wonder if we're good for ourselves.

Chapter Thirty

Ryder

I've never really been into Diet Dr. Pepper, but it tastes good on Virginia's tongue. Or maybe it's just her who tastes good.

I drop one of my hands to her waist and hold her. Let her be the one to kiss me, because it seems like she needs it.

And maybe I do, as well.

When the kiss ends, she's still holding my face. "I don't want the guy from the dream."

"Suck up," I tease her, but she doesn't laugh. Virginia and I might be different in many ways, but we're both grounded in reality—just a different reality. We know how the world works. We know everyone has their roles. As good as this feels right now, it probably won't last. She has her destiny and I have mine. The two probably won't mix.

"There's this…dance. Homecoming, at my school in a couple weeks. Hailey and Jamie are going with these guys, and… I could get you a guest pass."

When I step backward, her hands drop away.

When we first met, Virginia always looked at my lips when I spoke. Not because she wanted to kiss me, but because she wasn't used to my piercings. I've seen her school, and I know who she is there.

I wouldn't fit. It's not something I give a shit about for me, but for her. "I don't think that's really a good idea. They have to put where you go to school at things like that, right? They're not gonna want me there."

"So? *I* want you there. It's something I have to go to, Ryder. It's my senior year. It's important."

Translation: She's going with or without me.

"I get that." I shrug, but my insides are getting all tied up in knots. I don't want her to have to go without me. But shit like that takes money, which we both know I don't have. "I should get back in there." Bigger bullshit has never come out of my mouth. We both know there is zero reason for me to have to go back into the café.

"Fine." She jerks open her door.

"Hey. It's not you. I wanna dance with you." And I do. "But I can't…" I've often thought about meeting her dad and her friends, wanting to be a part of every aspect of her life, but how can I be when she doesn't even know who I am? Not everything, at least. Not the big stuff.

"Okay," she says. "I'll…I'll talk to you later." I can tell she's hurt, but still I let her get in the car. I don't stop her from starting it or tell her not to drive away. Instead, I let her go.

Even though it's cold out, my body feels like that one time Shane's car overheated, smoke coming out of the hood and all.

Suddenly, I'm pissed that she asked me and pissed I said no. Pissed that I have to go back into the diner to get my shit because

I know Luke will be waiting inside for me.

I make it all the way to the back table before Luke shows up. "Hey, you heading out?"

"Yeah, Shane will be here to get me in a bit." I'm a good liar. I always have been.

"You want something to eat first?"

Umm, what? Luke hasn't asked me to eat here in a long time. That's all it takes for me to realize why he's doing it. Because he saw me with Virginia? Saw me doing homework and being the good little boy so now I'm suddenly worthy? "Nah, it's cool."

"Listen." Luke rubs the back of his neck. "Do you have a minute? Can we go talk in the office?" He's wearing an *Annie's Café* T-shirt, stained from a day's work. It's so not Luke. For the first time, I wonder if he hates himself every day he puts it on. No, I guess it's me he hates since I'm the one he had to come back for.

"Shane will be here any minute."

"Just for a second, Ry. Please."

I don't remember the last time my brother said please to me. It's me who goes for the hallway first. I wait beside the office door for him to unlock it. He closes the door behind us and I fall into one of the chairs.

"The principal and I have been talking every day."

"What the fuck? You're keeping tabs on me?"

Luke shakes his head. "It's new. Since the last time you skipped school. You're my responsibility, Ry. That's what I'm here for."

No matter how much he hates it.

"He said you've been doing better lately. You haven't

173

skipped in weeks. Your teachers say you've been turning in your homework assignments. That girl…did she get through to you? Whatever it is, I'm proud of you."

I shove out of the chair. "Because of Virginia, of course. It has to be because of her. I would never want to do good on my own, right?"

"Hey, that's not what I said, but you have to admit you never tried before her. We're lucky you were on track to graduate!"

Tell me again, a voice inside my head whispers, *tell me you're proud of me.* I hate myself because of that voice. Hate that I want this from Luke. That I need it. He's never been proud of me before, never told me anything I did really mattered unless he was telling me how much I was ruining my life. How much Dad sucked and how I'd be just like him.

"I'm out of here." I make it to the door before his voice stops me.

"Don't go." His voice cracks. Luke steps toward me, popping his knuckles. He does that when he's nervous.

Still, he's the one who went first. He never wanted to stay for me, and now he wants to pretend he's close to me.

"I'm tired of fighting with you. I didn't want that. I just wanted to tell you I'm proud of you about school and everything. She's pretty, your girlfriend."

She wants me to go to homecoming at her school with her. I want to tell him, ask him what I should do, ask him to help. But the words get lost inside me.

"You really like her a lot." *Pop, pop, pop.*

I drop my forehead against the door. "Yeah."

"She lives in Cliffton. This big ass house with all this nice stuff. Her mom's a writer. I don't know what her dad does, but

174

it's something big. She gets straight A's and she's in FBLA. Do you know what that is? Future Business Leaders of America."

"Yeah," Luke says. "Yeah, I know."

Of course, he would.

"When you were doing your work, when you weren't looking at her, she was always looking at you. She likes you just as much as you like her, Ry. All that other stuff doesn't matter."

But it does, and *thank you,* war inside me.

"Does she know? About Dad and…"

Luke might not have the balls to, but I finish for him. "Me? No."

What am I supposed to tell her? My dad is a criminal by trade? He's on the run, and I used to do jobs with him? That I've been caught stealing twice since he left, though both times were a while ago? That I've only quit because if I get locked up, I can't go to Dad, and that I only have one more strike?

"All that shit? You were a kid. That's on Dad. You did what you were taught. But you're old enough to make your own decisions now, little bro. Whatever you do, I want you to know I'm proud of your behavior these past few weeks."

There has never been a day in my life I thought I was as good as Luke. I've never been as polite as him or as smart as he is. I've never been responsible like he was, even when he was too young to really understand the word. I've never done something to make him proud. *Proud.* That's the word I want lost inside me, so even when I can't remember it, it's always there— trapped. Maybe I'll still be able to feel it.

"I have to head back out there and get to work."

Slowly, I turn toward my brother. He leans against the desk. When I face him, he runs a hand through his dark hair.

"Can I...can I stay back here until you get off?"

He doesn't call me on the fact that I said Shane's coming. He just nods and says, "Of course. We'll ride home together."

And then he leaves me in the room, alone with my thoughts, alone with the knowledge of what I have to do.

Chapter Thirty-One
Virginia

It's been a couple days since I've seen Ryder. We've texted back and forth every day but haven't been able to catch up. My friends and I aren't organizing the Homecoming dance this year, but they've been asking for our help. When I add that on top of everything else I have going on, it cuts into my time.

I'm not sure what Ryder's doing today, and I miss him. It's ridiculous and lame. It's been three days. It's not like that's so long, but then I realize something—it's okay to miss a boy. It's okay to want to be with him as long as I still take care of myself. Which I am. It's the reason I'm driving out to Mom's right now.

I miss her, too.

The thing is, Mom has always pushed when it came to me. Just like she shoved her way into my room the day she came to my school, she's always pushed her way into my life, kept herself close.

Since our last argument, she hasn't pushed.

Hasn't called.

I haven't heard a word from her.

That's probably wrong of me, to want her here, to want her to call me or to come talk to me when I'm not sure I would be receptive of it. I kind of think that's what makes us human, though. We all have selfish feelings, whether we admit to them or not. We all want to be loved, even if we can't show we feel the same.

Right now, I want my mom. I want to tell her about Ryder and ask her what to do. I want to laugh with her, and whisper that I think I'm in love, and tell her how scary that is. There's even a part of me that wants her to know I want to be with him because he makes my nerve endings feel like they're shorting out due to too much electricity every time he touches me.

I want to know what her first time was like.

I want a guarantee that she'll always be 'her' when we speak.

My fingers linger on the key when I park across the street from her house. It's the house we all used to live in, where the dining room table used to be when we had our talks.

Closing my fingers, I turn the key, but don't get out of the car. I guess I knew when I came here that I wouldn't get out. From here, I can be close to her without the risk of all the other stuff.

Without seeing her fear and pain, and without being scared that I'll be just like her.

When I look at the house, I see the times I needed her, when she couldn't be there for me. I see when she left me alone for days to go to a concert—the little girl pretending she wasn't afraid, when that fear was the only thing that kept her blood pumping.

I see that girl looking at the woman who she loved and admired, and then experiencing her pain when she was let down time and time again.

My phone buzzes in my lap, pulling me out of the memories. When I look down, the screen is wet from my tears.

I'm tired of being a girl named Fear. Or a girl named Weak, Lonely, Destiny, Guilt or anything else. It's too much. They're too much. It's almost like I'm already not the person I want to be. I'm already not Virginia.

So I dry my eyes. Then my phone.

Can we meet at your place? Have some time before your dad gets home?

Ryder.

I don't hesitate to reply. **I'll be there in thirty.**

Chapter Thirty-Two

Ryder

Dad's hands always shook when he did a job. It never disrupted what he was doing, but they always trembled.

Once, I asked him if it was because he was scared. He was the man to me. I never imagined him being afraid of anything, so it didn't make sense.

Dad said it wasn't fear, it was excitement.

He loved the rush of being able to take what he wanted. Loved showing people who thought they were better than him that he always came out on top.

As fucked as it sounds, I wanted my hands to shake after that conversation.

Eventually they did, and I thought it was incredible.

Right now, I can't get them to stop, and I hate it. It's not excitement this time. It's fear. There's nothing I want more than for the earthquake to stop. I don't want to worry. I want to know everything will be okay.

Virginia pulls into her driveway and smiles at me. It's a lie, though. I see it in the shape of her lips and the way she holds her body. My voice echoes in my head—*What's wrong?* But I don't let the words pass my lips. If I do, I'll chicken out. It will be my excuse not to tell her. I may be a thief, but I'm not a liar.

"Hey." I open her door for her. "Hand me your bag. I'll carry it in for you." She does and then gets out. I close the door behind her.

My hand burns with the need to run it through her hair. It's the color of honey, hanging neat against her back.

"What's wrong?" Virginia cocks her head slightly and I wonder how she knows. How she sees something's wrong when I'm usually good at hiding it when I want to. Most of the time, I don't care enough to hide it.

And now I can't stop myself from threading my fingers through all the light brown. I let my hand rest on her neck as I lean forward and press my lips to her forehead. I want her mouth. Selfishly, I want to kiss her lips in case this is the last time; but that's not fair to her. Not telling her who I am was never fair to Virginia.

"Nothing." I nod toward her house. Let's go in.

I follow Virginia to the door. She unlocks it and then steps aside for me to go in first. She doesn't usually do that, and it will make this tougher, but I walk past her. As I step inside, I let a small cough out before slipping my hand into my pocket.

Virginia closes the door. I let her take the lead this time as she heads for the stairs. Instead of going up first, she waits. I let my hand slide across the table beside me as I walk. The next part will be tougher, but I have no doubt I'll pull it off. I stumble a little. Virginia grins but takes a step, making it so I'm behind her like I need to be so I can finish things off.

When we get to her room, I close the door and set her backpack on the bed.

"Can you believe I didn't do my homework right after school? That means we have to do it now. We can play the game, though. How many kisses for each assignment?"

Do it. Do homework with her and hold her and forget about everything else.

But I don't.

My hands start going crazy again. My throat gets tight, and I realize how ironic this is. I haven't even thought about stealing in so long. I haven't wanted to do it, but here I am and I now hate it. "Remember that night on the beach? When you asked me what I inherited from my dad?"

Her nose wrinkles. It's cute as hell. I've never thought something like that is cute on a girl before.

"Yeah…" The wheels are turning in her head. She's trying to figure out where I'm going with this.

For the millionth time, I want to forget it. Turn around and back off the edge. But I don't. I reach into my pocket and pull out the little gold box.

Virginia takes it, still looking lost. "It's supposed to hold good luck. You keep it by the door, so that anyone who walks in can 'take luck' if they need to."

"I didn't know that." I shrug, wishing I could have taken some luck from it as I picked it off the table when we walked in.

Again, my hand slides into my pocket. This time I pull out the brown leather case that holds pens. It was on top of the journals on the table at the foot of the stairs.

Her eyes, full of questions, go wide like they were the first night. I love the crazy shade of green, but hate the uncertainty I see in them now.

"I don't understand what you're telling me."

Because she doesn't want to see it.

My heart starts slam-dancing against my ribs, break-dancing the way Tanner does. The echo in my ears is so loud I can hardly hear. One more reach into my other pocket. This time I pull out her wallet. The wallet that was in the front zipper on her backpack before I carried it for her.

She always keeps it there.

"How…" Virginia takes a step backward but her bed stops her. "I didn't hear anything. Not the zipper or… You walked in in front of me. How did you get the luck box without me seeing it… Why?" She shakes her head.

On instinct, I step forward, wanting to comfort her. To tell her I'm sorry and that it will be okay. I *am* sorry, but I don't really know if it will be okay. And right now, I don't deserve to touch her.

"My dad's a criminal." I shrug as though it doesn't matter. "He's a thief, as in, it's what he does. He taught me when I was young, and I was good at it. It's the only thing I've ever really been good at. He's actually wanted right now. It's how Luke got stuck with me. He always said he'd come back for me." And for the first time, I wonder if I'll really want to go with him… Virginia has college and I have Dad, but the thought of going creates a hole in my chest. Tasting the words I just spoke to her makes me want to vomit.

Virginia doesn't reply. Her legs go out. I step forward again but stop myself. She falls to the bed, silent.

"He used to take me on jobs with him. When he left, I got caught shoplifting twice. I stole a car when I was fourteen to try and find my dad, only I didn't get caught that time. I have two strikes. I can't get another one before I turn eighteen or I go to juvie."

Talk... Say something. But what would she say? That I'm a piece of shit? Maybe it's true. That what I've done is wrong? I know that already. There's nothing she can really say.

"I've never taken anything from you, though. Today…that was just to show you. I didn't plan to keep it. I'd never steal from you, and I haven't done it in a long time. I haven't even wanted to." Like that's supposed to make it better.

No reply. Nothing.

I'm sorry... "So yeah… We talked about destinies before, and that's mine…"

It's those words that make her head jerk up and her eyes latch onto me again. My body gets jittery, like I have to fight myself to keep from going to her. From putting my arms around her and asking her to tell me it's okay. Even if it's a lie.

"My dad's an attorney. Did I ever tell you that?"

Fuck. I don't think she's telling me this because she thinks I'll hire him to represent me. It's her way of saying they do the right thing. They're *good.* They don't take shit from other people and then complain about how the world has wronged them.

Which is exactly what my dad does

And I always have, too.

"I…I need some time, Ryder. This is a lot to take in."

After dropping that bomb, I'm lucky she's only asking for time instead of telling me never to talk to her again.

"I don't know if I'm okay with this."

She's not. Even I know that. And she shouldn't be.

"It's cool… I mean, it's not cool. What I did isn't cool. I get it. I just needed to be honest before this goes any further."

I make it to her bedroom door before I stop. Without turning to look at her, I say, "I know you're better than this. It's why I was scared to tell you. No matter what, I understand, okay? Don't feel bad because you do the right thing, Virginia. It's what I like most about you."

With that, I leave to start the long walk home.

Chapter Thirty-Three
Virginia

Over, and over I roll my phone around in my hand. It's a pretty sad thing that I don't have someone to call. Or maybe not. How many girls want to tell their friends or their mom that the boy they're dating can pocket anything and she's never even known it? That he steals as easily as he…walks up the stairs? Because I hadn't noticed a thing. Not when he walked past me into the house or anything.

My boyfriend is a thief. Not only that, but his dad is on the run. Ryder didn't sound like he knew where his father was, but what if he does? And what happens if he comes back for Ryder?

I would have a boyfriend who is running from the cops with his father. What if I'm put in a position to be an accomplice, where I'd have to turn him in or it's on me too?

That's not something I can do…

A stiffness sets into my muscles. I can't breathe, can't move. My body is torn between seizing up or purging everything Ryder told me so we can go back to the way things were before.

The only thing is, I can't do that.

It's not me.

He's the first boy to make me feel normal. The first boy I know who would never judge me if he learned my family curse. The boy who I can trust, because even though I know he has to be curious, he hasn't gone digging into the things Mom said.

Not if he told me he didn't.

When I hear the door downstairs, I stumble out of bed. I'm supposed to be making dinner tonight, yet I haven't done anything. My whole afternoon has been spent stalking Mom's house and being depressed about Ryder.

Get it together, Lu.

My eyes catch the table at the base of the stairs as I walk down.

When he stumbled... That has to be when he got my wallet, because then he was behind me. He had the whole thing planned out, knew exactly what to do.

Oh, God.

"Hi, Lulu. Hey, what's wrong?" Dad asks.

Not without a struggle, I school my features. "Um, nothing. I didn't cook. I had a lot of homework and just finished."

I guess it's time to change my name to Liar again.

"That's okay, kiddo. Do you want to order pizza?" He ruffles my hair, and the urge to follow him to his office and climb into his lap hits me. I used to love sitting on my dad's lap in his office. It's so orderly. I always felt secure within those walls.

"Sure."

"I'm going to go change. I'll be right back down."

While Dad goes upstairs, I order the pizza. He's back a few minutes later. This is normally where I would go upstairs. My dad and I are close, but it's not like we hang out while I'm home or anything. Unless I need order. That's when I sit in his office with him. Only, it doesn't feel right today. Right now, I just want someone to hug me.

Forty-five minutes. That's how long I wander around downstairs—sit at the table, stand up, sit in the chair, turn on the TV, turn it back off, stand up again. Walk to Dad's office, don't go in, head to the kitchen, over and over and over.

Finally, the doorbell rings, giving me something to do.

We have a credit card that's in both mine and Dad's name for stuff like this. That's what I use to pay for dinner. When I close the door behind the pizza man, Dad's stepping up beside me and taking the double pepperoni, double cheese from my hand.

"You didn't get one for you?" He winks at me.

"Ha ha."

Dad sets the pizza on the dining room table. I fill two glasses of Diet Dr. Pepper while he grabs plates. A few minutes later, he's finished his first piece and I'm poking around at mine. "Can I ask you something?" By the time the words finish coming out of my mouth, I'm still not sure what I'm going to say.

"Anything. All the time. You know that." Dad sets his slice down and gives me all his attention.

Both my parents are like that, and for a second, I wonder if Ryder's dad was. If he would listen to Ryder and care what he said. I wonder what kind of father takes his son out with him when he steals.

"What made you go into defense? You know, instead of prosecution or something. Why do you want to defend people who have done things wrong?" Dad is the best person I've ever known. He's loyal and honest. He's levelheaded and caring. Despite everything, Mom is still his best friend. He would never wrong or hurt anyone. It feels like he should want to put bad guys in jail, not keep them out.

"Why do you assume they've all done something wrong, Lulu? That's not always the case."

Which I know. I get it. Not everyone accused of a crime committed it.

I poke at my pizza. "What if they did, though? What if they did it and you know? Or what if you're not sure. People lie all the time. What if you trust someone, believe in them, and you're wrong?"

Dad gives me a sad smile, pushes his glasses higher on his nose, and says, "Then I'm human. We're all wrong every once in a while, kiddo."

"What I don't understand is why someone would want to risk that. Risk putting their faith into someone if there's a chance they could be wrong."

"The thing is, Lulu, believing in people, trusting and putting ourselves out there, those are some of the most basic, human things you can do. They give you empathy. They help you understand people who are different from you. And the truth is, I don't think everyone who makes a mistake is bad."

I look up as he continues.

"There are so many extenuating circumstances you have to take into consideration. Like your mom…she's hurt you, and she's hurt me, but it wasn't her fault. What she's gone through…people live things every day that others know nothing about. It's easy to stand on the outside and cast judgment."

Which I've done. I know that.

"But how do you know? What if you believe in someone and you're wrong?"

"You *don't* know. You have to trust your gut and your heart. You have to look at as much of the picture as you can. I've defended people who had terrible childhoods, who felt like they had no way out, and who screwed up. And once I helped them, once I showed them someone cares, they turned their lives around. Sometimes that's all it takes. Some of the people I've helped have gone on to do great things; they've gone on to help other people.

"And some of them have gone on to do bad things again. I have no way of knowing. I try to ask myself if I really think the client is a good person or not. I take into account their history, as well. And of course, the crime matters. Do I want to help free a man who attacked a woman, or someone who hurt a child? Of course not. There have been times I did the wrong thing, kiddo. But there have been others where I did the right one…and *that* is a wonderful feeling."

I saw the shame in Ryder's eyes when he handed me each of the objects from his pocket today. I hear the words he's said to me in the past…about people not believing in him, assuming the worst of him, and just today, that stealing was the only thing he'd ever been good at.

He's wrong about that. He's a good friend to Drea, Shane, Tanner and Cody. He's smart and funny, and maybe even a little noble.

And I believe in him. Just like how Dad always believed in Mom. That doesn't mean we don't have things to figure out. It doesn't mean I will be with someone who steals. But I believe in him.

Pushing to my feet, I walk over to Dad and hug him. He squeezes me back, and doesn't let go until I do. "Thank you."

"Do you want to tell me where all this is coming from?"

I shake my head.

"Teenagers… I didn't think so. Sit down, finish eating with me."

So I do, for the first time in a long time, thankful for this dining room table and a talk we had at it.

I refuse to believe following in his dad's footsteps is Ryder's destiny.

That leaves me with one last question…what about my own destiny?

Chapter Thirty-Four

Ryder

My phone died hours ago. I'd hardly had any juice left in it when I texted Virginia to meet. I've taken back roads, sort of wandering around all night. There's a lot that can go through your mind when you're alone at night. It's like a fucking freight train or something that doesn't want to stop as it circles my brain.

I think about the people Dad has stolen from. He used to tell me that in the grand scheme of things, they were people who would never miss the money, and their stuff was insured. Oh, it might piss them off that someone dared to mess with them, but they had so much stuff it didn't matter.

Like Robin Hood, except the poor was us. We robbed from them for ourselves.

These were people who would never give a shit about us, so why should we care about them?

Tonight, I wonder if I ever really believed that, or if I just told myself I did to feel better.

Virginia is the type of person he would see as one of the "haves," but I know her. It doesn't matter that her parents have money; she cares. She's the girl who bought me a hoodie because I didn't have one.

The owner of the bar they robbed when I was the lookout…he was a small-business owner. As a kid, that didn't mean anything to me, but I look at the owners of the diner Luke runs. After they pay everything each month, they hardly have more than we do.

Still we took from people like them, businesses like theirs. After Dad left, I did it on my own—more than the two times I was caught. I stole and wrecked someone's car. Maybe it was their only way to get to work so they could feed their family.

My gut cramps up and I hold it. If there was anything in it, I have no doubt I would lose it all over the road. I was a thief. I was wrong.

And if it wasn't for Virginia, I never would have seen this. Does that still make me blind? If I'm too screwed in the head to see past myself until someone else shows me there's more?

I don't know.

Pushing my hands back into my pockets, I turn down my driveway. The sun is just starting to come up. It shouldn't have taken me all night to walk from Virginia's, but I hadn't been in a hurry—hadn't taken the easiest route, either.

My eyelids feel like they've been replaced with sandpaper. My muscles with cement, and my bones with rubber. Luke's going to kick my ass, because there's no way I can go to school today. At least he'll know up front, so it will be an excused absence.

My key turns in the lock but it's already open so I just push. I didn't even notice the lights in the windows until it shines in my eyes when I open the door. Luke stops mid-step in the living room. He's fully dressed, looking tense as hell.

My heart does this swoop and accelerate thing. "What's wrong—umpf." I stumble backward when Luke throws his arms around me. He knocks me into the door, pushing it closed.

My pulse picks up even quicker—Oh, shit. They caught Dad. He's in trouble…or worse.

"Luke, what happened?" I try to pull away from my brother but he's still holding on to me.

It's not until he whispers, "Don't ever fucking do that to me again, Ry," that I realize this isn't about Dad. It's about me. Luke was worried about me. And he's hugging me. When's the last time my brother hugged me?

It's then that I go flying back. He shoves me into the wall. "What the hell were you thinking? You've been gone all night. Your phone goes straight to voicemail. Shane, Drea, Tanner and Cody didn't know where you were. Virginia said you guys got into an argument."

Wait. What? "You talked to Virginia?"

"That's all you got out of this?" Luke shakes his head. He's texting on his phone as he speaks. "We've been worried about you. Everyone has been looking for you all night. I was just pissed at first, thinking you were off pouting about something, but then Shane came looking for you. We realized no one knew where you were, so Drea had to go to Virginia's."

Oh shit. "Dre went to Virginia's?" Now I'm the one pacing.

"We didn't know what the hell else to do! No one had her number so Drea pretended to be a friend from school, knocking on her door at eleven thirty at night."

It's as though my thoughts are arguing with each other, trying to decide what's more important here. The fact that all these people were worried about me? That Luke was, or that they dragged Virginia into it? She'd just asked for time, and now one of my best friends, who I happened to have kissed on too many occasions to count, goes to her house at eleven thirty on a school night?

Her dad is going to hate me...

Virginia probably already does.

"I can't believe you pulled this shit." Anger blazes in Luke's eyes.

"I didn't...I didn't mean to. I wasn't trying to be a dick. Virginia and I...I told her about Dad, and she said she needed some time, and I just... I screwed it up with her and I didn't know what to do, so I walked. My phone was dead."

That's when the anger seeps from his expression. Luke frowns, looking at me...I don't know, in a way he's never looked at me before. "You told her about Dad?"

It's not like it's a big secret. Shane and Drea know. Cody and Tanner do as well, so I'm not sure why Luke is acting like it's such a big deal.

Doors slam, one after another, outside. They echo through me. Is one of them Virginia? As though he can read my thoughts, Luke nods his head at the door. I jerk it open. My feet hardly hit the gravel at the foot of the stairs before Virginia's running at me. She rams into me harder than Luke did, throwing her arms around my neck.

I hardly catch her, but manage to get my arms around her waist and hold her.

"I'm sorry. All I could think was that it was my fault. You told me something big and I just let you go, let you *walk* away.

That was so irresponsible of me. No matter how shocked I was, I should have driven you home."

Each of her words, seeds of hope, plants themselves inside my chest. She cares. Even if she can't be with me anymore, she knows what I've done, and she cares.

"Hey. It's okay. I'm right here. Nothing happened to me. I was just being an idiot and walked from Cliffton. My phone died. That's all. And it wasn't your fault."

Looking over her shoulder, I realize she's not the only one here. Both her car and Shane's are parked out front. Shane, Tanner and Cody are leaning against Shane's ride. When my eyes land on the window, I realize someone's sitting inside.

Drea.

Virginia's hold on me loosens, and then it's gone. "She was really worried about you… She kept trying to hide it, but she was crying."

My eyes close. This is the second time I've made Drea cry. My chest feels like someone cracked it open. I love her. I'm not *in* love with her, but Dre is my friend. I feel like such an ass.

"You should go see her." Virginia takes a step back. I'm tethered between the two of them—not wanting to hurt either of them, but in different ways. Virginia because I don't want her to think there's more between me and Drea, and Dre because I know she loves us all so much. Shane, me, Tanner and Cody are her family.

"She's one of my best friends," I tell Virginia. Even if she can't be with me anymore, I want to make sure she doesn't think there's more to it.

"I know." And then she walks over to the porch stairs and sits down. With a sigh, I turn to my friends.

Chapter Thirty-Five

Virginia

There once was a girl named Fake. Her favorite holiday was Halloween. She loved it so much, she pretended it was Halloween every day. She'd dress in different costumes and give herself different names, because it was easier than trying to figure out who she really was. Was she Perfect or Lonely? Fear or Destiny?

She couldn't decide so she smiled to cover the lie, and said, "Happy Halloween" when people asked her who she was. No matter how hard she tried, she just couldn't see a clear reflection. Was she the girl who told her boyfriend he should go to his friend, and then sat back wishing he hadn't gone? Was she the girl who thought she was confident and strong, only to realize again that her name was Weak as she watched him hug the girl who wanted a house inside his heart?

Or was she the girl who let stories run around in her head, but would never risk putting them on paper? Because if no one read them, she could deny they existed. Deny that words lived inside her the way they had her Mom and her Grandmother, and Virginia Woolf. Deny that she liked the way they felt as they coasted along her brain waves. Creating. Living.

There once was a girl named Denial.

~*~

Ryder stands in the driveway as his friends pile into Shane's car and drive away.

A hand lands on my shoulder, a voice behind me. "Thank you…for coming. For caring about my brother."

Something lodges in my throat and I wonder when I became so emotional. Why I'm always feeling so much. Words can't seem to make their way around the block, so Luke squeezes my shoulder again, and then I hear the door to the house close.

Ryder walks my way and holds out his hand. "Let's sit in your car. I don't want Luke to hear us, but I don't want you cold, either."

He has to be exhausted. He's been up, walking all night. I'd gotten a little sleep before Drea showed up—when I thought Ryder was ignoring my phone calls.

Taking his hand, I step in front of him; lead the way to my car. I sit behind the wheel, Ryder in the passenger seat.

"Are you going to get into trouble for sneaking out?" he asks.

"No. I didn't. I told my dad that I had a friend who needed me…. That I was going to her house. He trusts me."

"What about school?"

"I'll go in late."

"Did Drea give you shit? She's hurt…not that that excuses it. I screwed up with her—you, too. I didn't want anyone to get hurt."

And he didn't. I know that. "We didn't really talk. She came to my door to get me, and then she went with Shane and Tanner. Cody came with me."

Ryder sighs. "I'm sorry. Not just for last night, but for everything. I should have told you before you got wrapped up with me...I mean, if you are wrapped up with me. I guess you were, but—"

"I want you to go to Homecoming with me." Ugh. I didn't mean to blurt that out like that.

"What?" He cocks his head.

"Wait." I wring my hands together. "That's not what I wanted to start with. I don't believe that's your destiny...being like your dad. That's not who I see when I look at you. You could have taken things from my house a million times—"

"I wouldn't. I'd never take anything from you," Ryder cuts me off.

"I know. I trust you...but I'm not stupid, either. I can't be that person who throws herself into a situation blindly. I need to know if that's who you *want* to be, Ryder—if you don't see anything wrong with it, or if you can't promise me you won't steal again, then no matter how much I want to be with you, I can't. And it can't be that you just won't take things from me; you can't take them from anyone."

If he can't assure me of that, I have to walk away. I *will* walk away, and then I'll be the girl I never wanted to be—the one who gets her heart broken in high school.

There are certain things I can't sacrifice, though, and not being able to trust him, thinking he's the guy who's going to take something from others rather than working for it, is one of those things.

Chapter Thirty-Six

Ryder

Sometimes you think you want something specific, and then something else, or someone else, comes along and blows that all to hell. A few weeks ago, if someone would have told me that a girl would give me an ultimatum about not doing something—any kind of something—or they couldn't be with me, I would have said, see ya later.

The thing is with Virginia that's not what it feels like. Don't get me wrong, she'll walk away if she thinks I'm jacking stuff. That much I can guarantee. But it doesn't feel like she's telling me to choose—who I am or being with her—it feels like she's letting me decide who I am. Like she's giving me a chance to be that person. Like maybe she sees more in me than I ever have.

It's funny, the difference in someone telling you who you are or who you should be and someone leaving that decision up to you. It makes you see options instead of rebelling. Maybe it even helps you see truths.

"My dad always said there's a balance to the world. The world wouldn't work with only people like you; they need people like me to counter them. To keep things going."

"We're the same kind of people, Ryder." And then she lays her head on my shoulder. It's familiar. I know the feel of her hair against my face and the smell of her skin. I never want to stop knowing it.

"I don't want what Dad said… I don't want to be the guy who can slip things in my pocket without someone knowing, the one who can hotwire a car in thirty seconds flat."

"You can hotwire a car?"

I pause, not really wanting to give her any reason to question her decision, but not able to lie to her, either. "Yeah. I told you yesterday that I've stolen a car."

I don't have to see her to know she closed her eyes. "I must have blanked that part out."

"I've taken cars on a joyride that aren't mine. There's a lot of things I've done. But I won't anymore. I promise you. It's not who I want to be. I didn't realize that until recently. I…" want to be the guy my brother doesn't want to run away from. The one he respects. The guy Virginia can respect as well. I want to be able to meet her dad and for him to like me. I don't want to be the guy who thinks he can take whatever he wants without working for it. "I think I'm in love with you."

And yeah, that sounded totally lame, but I don't even care. It's true.

Virginia gasps. Her head shoots off my shoulder but I just shake my head. "Don't say anything back. Not yet. I know you have to go to school in a few hours. Are you sure you're not too tired to drive home? I can drive you. Maybe Luke can follow us out and take me back home or something."

She looks up at me; all green eyes and a smile. "You're

changing everything, and I can't figure out why I'm not more scared about that."

I press my lips to her forehead. "Yeah, me either."

She's in her car with the engine started, before I remember something. I knock on the window and Virginia lowers it. "Are you sure you want me there? At your school? This is me, Virginia. The outside isn't going to change."

"Who said I want it to?" With a wink, she drives away.

And I'm fucking happy. Happy about a *dance*. Happy I told her the truth. Happy I'm with her. And scared of screwing up.

Luke's waiting on the couch when I get inside. His eyes pop open and I can tell he'd almost been asleep.

Guilt wrestles around in my stomach. "I didn't know you'd be worried."

He sighs. "Of course I'd be worried, Ryder."

Shoving my hands into the pocket of my hoodie, I walk over and fall to the couch beside him. "Sorry."

Leaning back, I close my eyes too, half because I'm tired, half because it's hard to look at him sometimes. "I need a job, man. You think I can get one at the diner? Washing dishes or something?"

The couch shifts, telling me he's sitting up. "Why do you need a job? You've never wanted to get one before."

I shrug. "Virginia... I'm supposed to take her to the Homecoming dance at her school." Opening my eyes, I roll my head on the back of the couch so I can see him. "She goes to a private school in Cliffton... I got dinner to worry about, and clothes. I'm gonna need to wear a suit or something. Oh, and that wrist flower thing. It's bad enough she's going to have to drive; I need to make sure I do the other stuff for her."

Luke's quiet, his eyes a scalpel performing surgery. He's dissecting me, trying to figure me out. I shift and look away, not wanting to know what he sees. "I only have a couple weeks. It's probably not enough time to get a job and get paid, but I need to try."

It takes Luke at least a minute to reply. My body is a weird mixture of tenseness and resignation. He's going to tell me he can't get me a job.

"I'll make you a deal, Ryder."

This time, it's me who studies him. "What kind of deal?"

"What if you just focus on school right now? Keep going every day like you have been, turn in your work every day and all that. That's what's more important right now—school. If you keep up your end of the bargain, and don't get into any trouble, then I'll make sure you have everything you need for the dance. And…" he shrugs. "I'll even let you take my car. I know it's kind of a piece of shit, but it'll be yours for the night and you can drive her."

I almost ask him to repeat everything he just said because I can't make myself believe it. Luke is always stressing about money, so dropping a few hundred on a dance isn't something we can afford. And he never, ever lets me drive his car. I've never been able to take it out without him.

"How?"

"Let me worry about the money. We both know it'll be legit. Do you think this sounds like a good idea? Do you want to do well in school in exchange for me helping you with the dance?"

I think it's the first time Luke's ever asked my opinion on something like this.

And I also know he's going to work his ass off picking up

extra shifts to get the money for me. "Are you sure?"

"Absolutely."

"Maybe after…I can get a job or something. You know, to help out, or whatever."

Luke shakes his head. "You're almost eighteen so I can't really stop you, but I'd rather you focus on finishing high school. You have the rest of your life to work."

It reminds me of what Virginia said her dad believes in. He doesn't want her to work while she's in school. Luke is telling me the same thing. It's almost like he's being a dad. The kind of dad Virginia has.

"Do you think you can give me a ride to school today? I don't know if Shane and them are going, and I feel like shit asking them after last night. I'm sure you're tired, too, but—"

"Of course." Luke nods toward my room. "Go get ready. I'll be out here waiting for you."

I get up and make it all the way to my door before I stop. "Hey, Luke?"

"Yeah?"

"Thanks."

Chapter Thirty-Seven

Virginia

It's been a strange few weeks. Ryder and I are trying to navigate our relationship after what he told me. I just want to forget it. I know what he's done and I want to move on, but I can tell it's harder for him. I feel like he's always trying to prove himself, and yeah, it makes me feel special, but it's not what I want from him.

In other ways, we feel more solid, more comfortable than before. I think maybe that's what truth does sometimes; it opens up your heart to someone, even if that truth originally hurt.

The dance has been a heavy weight hanging between us. He asked about the color of my dress—sea-foam green; Jamie says it looks great with my eyes—and where I wanted to go for dinner. It's so hard finding the right thing to say—to let him know that I realize money is tight and I don't need something big without making him feel bad, either.

Homework is much easier to understand than boys.

And we've been doing that a lot, even more homework than usual.

Now, I'm sitting in my car in front of his house, my stomach full of acidy nerves, the past few weeks a powerful waterfall in my brain.

My name is Liar again. My dad thinks I'm going to the dance with my friends.

It switches to Guilt because I'm scared to introduce Ryder to him.

Now I'm Fear, because he said he loved me that day and I haven't said it back. Even though I do. I love Ryder, and I want to be with him completely, which makes my fear even stronger.

Maybe I already am like my mom, different people in one body.

My eyes dart to the window when there's a little knock on it. Ryder's there. He nods backward like he's telling me to get out. A small smile teases his lips, only the left side tilted up almost…nervous.

But that's not what has me entranced…okay, not the *only* thing. Ryder in a suit is gorgeous.

He's still the same Ryder—still with the two piercings in his bottom lip. The same longish, messy black hair that's slightly wavy. The same mismatched eyes. In many ways, he still doesn't look like one single boy at my school. There's a roughness to him, a different look in his eyes, like he's seen more than anyone I know…but he looks softer, as well. Like he doesn't know just how good he looks.

He nods backward again, and then tugs on the collar of his suit as though it's annoying him. My breath catches in my throat.

Obviously tired of waiting for me, Ryder opens the door. I get out, and suddenly wish I would have had him pick me up at home. That he could have come to my door, and met my dad.

"Hey," he says, almost shyly when I get out of my car.

"Hey, yourself."

"You look…" He eyes me from head to toe, and I swear I feel it. Ryder puts a hand on my right side, fingers the fabric of my short dress where it dips at my waist. He brushes his other hand over my shoulders that are bare, and I shiver. He wraps one of the tendrils of hair that I left hanging in front around his finger. Most of my hair is tied back in a bun, but I had Hailey leave a few random curls because I like it when he touches them. "Like the most beautiful girl in the world."

"Wow…" I don't mean for the word to come out, but seriously, a compliment like that? How can I not be in shock by it?

"Didn't sound like me? How about…Holy shit, you're hot." Ryder winks and I laugh.

"Holy shit, you're hot, too."

"Whoa… Watch your language or I'm going to think I'm a bad influence on you. Come on. Luke wants to see us."

A pang lands in my gut. I'm the thief now, a girl named Thief because I stole these moments from both Mom and Dad— pictures of me going to Homecoming with the boy I love.

Ryder grabs my hand and leads me to the front porch. Luke is standing there with his cell phone. He takes a few pictures and Ryder grumbles the whole time.

I don't.

"Can you text those to Ryder so I can have them?" I ask his brother.

"Yeah, of course. No problem." And then he looks at Ryder. Luke hands him keys and then nods at him. Ryder returns it, and I know they're passing a million silent messages between them.

"Do you mind if we leave your car here, and I drive? I know

yours is better than Luke's, but—"

"No. I don't mind, I mean." I make a quick stop at my car for my sneakers. I don't walk well in heels, and the second the dance is over, I'll want to take them off.

We're quiet most of our drive to the restaurant. My friends asked us to go to dinner with them, but I figured maybe it would be easier if we went alone—kind of work into the evening, because I know this isn't going to be easy for Ryder.

I hope he has fun. Jamie and Hailey are my best friends. I want him to like them, even though they couldn't be more different from his friends.

Dinner isn't much better. First he realizes he forgot the corsage, then he spills his water, gets irritated and cusses too loud. An old couple from the table next to us shakes their heads at him.

"What, you don't curse?" I ask them, which makes Ryder's eyes go wide. The couple looks away.

By the time we get to the dance, I'm about ready to tell him he doesn't have to go. "I don't want this to be torture for you. Maybe it was a stupid idea…"

"I don't do this kind of shit, Virginia. I've never gone to one of my school dances. I just…I want tonight to be perfect for you."

That's when I realize what's wrong. I'm not a girl named Perfect, and I don't need the night to be that, either. Turning in the passenger seat, I click on the interior light. The dinner, my corsage, the suit… "You don't need to make this night perfect for me. I don't want you to try and be someone else, because…because I'm in love with the person you really are."

It's almost like someone hit a button, making Ryder's

movements slow-motion. He looks up from whatever he'd been focused on. There's a storm in his eyes that I can't read. I want to shelter him from it.

"I love you, too." His hand cups my cheek, and for the first time tonight, he kisses me. My tongue traces his piercings before slipping into his mouth. And then he's tasting me, and I'm tasting him, and I want to tell him he did what he said. He made tonight perfect.

Chapter Thirty-Eight

Ryder

The girls at the door taking tickets look at me funny but I don't care.

The building is decked out and decorated like the president is coming or something, but I don't let that bother me, either. I'm where I want to be, at my girl's side, and screw anyone who has a problem with it.

"Your school is ridiculous," I whisper in Virginia's ear.

"So you told me before; and we're not even at the school."

"Yeah, but your school *did* this. My school probably doesn't even have a yearly budget as big as yours for this one dance."

We're walking through the room. Music is blasting through the speakers. People are dancing, standing, sitting, talking, and I'm just going with her. I have no idea where.

"I have been responsible for putting on most of these, you know."

I bump her hip so she knows I'm joking. "Then you're

ridiculous, too."

"Lulu!" A girl screams and it takes me a minute to figure out they're talking to Virginia. How can anyone call her Lulu? It's not her.

"I knew they'd find me the second we got here. My friends are freaking out to meet you." There's a slight tremble to her voice. I get it. I was a little freaked when she met my friends.

"Do we have time to run?"

Two girls skid to a stop in front of us as Virginia says, "No."

And then they stare at me. I have no clue what the hell their looks mean, but I'm pretty sure it's not good.

"Hey." I nod. "They're piercings. They're supposed to be there."

"Ryder!" Virginia slaps my arm, but I hear the laugh in her voice. Two guys stand behind her friends; their dates, I'm assuming.

"Ryder, this is Jamie," she points to the girl with dark skin and braids. "And this is Hailey. Behind them are Juan and Danny. Guys, this is Ryder."

"Nice to meet you guys." The girls are still in some kind of trance so I shake Danny, then Juan's, hand. "What's up, man?"

"What's up?" they each reply, right before Hailey speaks.

"Your eyes are two different colors! That's so cool."

As soon as she says that, I know everything is going to be okay.

Virginia and I sit with them at their table. The girls start talking about colors and decorations, and that's when I zone out. Then, they do that thing I will never understand—they all go to the bathroom together.

There's never once been a time I asked Shane, Tanner or Cody to take a piss with me.

"Do you live around here?" Juan asks.

I scratch my forehead before replying. "Yeah, in Henderson. Not too far from here." Might as well be the other side of the world, though.

"Where'd you and Lulu meet? We didn't even know she was with anyone until her friends told Mike not to ask her to the dance."

I look at Danny as Juan elbows him. "Nice, man. Mike asked someone else. It's not a big deal."

It's not something I'm worried about so I don't comment on that. "The beach."

Arms wrap around my neck from behind. "Dance with me," Virginia says as her girlfriends go, "Awww!"

This school is so fucking weird.

"I'm not really a dancer." Still, I stand up. "Tanner's the one who does that."

"I heard." We find an empty space on the floor.

"Yeah, he's totally into it. Mostly break dancing and hip hop, but he knows a little bit of it all."

The longer we dance, the tighter the stupid collar feels around my neck. I would do anything to take this suit off. How in the hell do the other guys here not seem bothered by theirs?

It's fun watching Virginia dance. She lets go. She's not the girl who is obsessed with her homework or all the ways she needs to be responsible. She's...free. I want to be free with her.

Every so often we go sit with her friends but it is never long before she wants to dance again. I'm at the table with Juan and

Danny when the girls take Virginia to go dance by themselves. Her hair is starting to fall out of the tie-thing. It's a little wet with sweat around the edges, but I like that. Like she's having so much fun she's working up a sweat.

Jamie whispers something to Virginia, who nods her head excitedly. Hailey says something next and they all drop their heads back and laugh. I swear I feel the vibrations from it floating on the airwaves to me.

"I don't think they even need us here," Danny says.

"No shit." But that's okay. It's cool seeing her in her element—with her friends, at something for her school. I didn't know that part of her until tonight.

"They'll be announcing the Homecoming King and Queen soon. I'm sure it will be Mike and Lulu."

At that, I whip my head toward Juan, my muscles seizing up a bit. "Really?" I don't know whether that's cool or not. Actually, I do. If that's what Virginia wants, I hope she gets it. I just sort of wish it wouldn't be with that Mike guy.

This time, Danny replies. "Yeah. I'm sure his new girlfriend isn't real stoked about that, either."

"Nah, I'm cool." Kind of. Not because I don't trust her or would be pissed at her, but because I'll never be that person.

The music cuts out. "Alright, ladies and gentlemen, it's the moment we've all been waiting for. It's time to announce your Homecoming King and Queen!"

Virginia stops what she's doing, looks at me, and then walks my way. She knows it might be her.

"Why didn't you tell me?" I ask her when she reaches me.

"I didn't want to give you a reason not to come... I'm sorry. That was wrong." And then she mumbles something that sounds like, "There once was a girl named Fear…"

"Hey, com'ere." I pull her to my chest. My chin rests on her head, and I'm holding her. "It's cool… I just might have to kick his ass after the dance." Her chest vibrates against mine and I know she's laughing. I love that she doesn't freak out, that she knows when I'm kidding.

That she doesn't pull away or ask me to let her go as whoever the guy who's talking opens up an envelope like we're at the fucking Oscars or something.

"Ladies first… Your senior class Homecoming Queen is Lulu Nichols!"

Seriously, what the hell is up with this school? I feel like I'm in a movie or something. They spotlight us. I kiss her forehead and she squeezes me before letting go. Everyone is clapping, and the light follows her as she walks up to the stage. The old guy up there puts a crown on her head, and she smiles. Then my hands are hitting together and I'm clapping for her, too.

I sort of blur out after that. They call the Mike guy's name and everyone cheers for him. He gets another fucked up crown, and then they say it's time for the King and Queen to dance.

Oh. I didn't know about that part.

Virginia locks eyes with me and I see it there. She's unsure what to do, but I know her. She doesn't want to cause a scene…and she shouldn't. Not over this. It's one stupid dance, so I nod and clap louder, even though I suddenly wish I really could kick Mike's ass.

There's space between them. She doesn't hold him tight or put her head against his chest or anything like that, but it still makes my heart hurt to see her with him. Because she fits with the douchebag. He's the guy who wouldn't have to make a screwed up deal with his brother to go to school and do his homework just so he could afford to take her to the dance.

But then…there's a part of me who is sort of proud I did that as well. Proud Luke offered, and proud it was important enough to me to accept.

The song ends and it moves into another slow one. This one's mine. I head her way just as she turns to me. I smile at her so she doesn't think I'm pissed or hurt because of the dance.

"I get the rest of them." I pull her close.

"I'm sorry."

"Don't be. You're holding me way tighter than you did him." And she is. I let my hands touch all the skin I can on her shoulders and upper back. I move them up and down her spine, touching dress now as her hands fist in my suit.

"Thank you, Ryder."

"For what?" I ask her.

"Everything. Tonight was perfect. What…what are your friends doing tonight? I want to hang out with them, the way you hung out with mine…and then…my dad isn't expecting me home tonight. I told him I'm staying with Jamie."

Holy. Shit. Is she saying what I think she is? "You can…if you want to. Stay with Jamie."

"I don't…want to."

Thank God. "Okay, sure. Whatever you want. I can sneak you past Luke, and if you want, I can stay on the couch or whatever. Just let me know, okay?" Because I don't want to push her. I don't want her to think I expect anything.

But she stops dancing and looks right into my eyes. "I don't want you on the couch."

Chapter Thirty-Nine

Virginia

Ryder drives to a house that's in the middle of nowhere. It's closer to his house than it is mine. We're still in the car, and the music from the house is so loud I'm vibrating.

"I'm cool if you want to go somewhere else." The car is still running and I shake my head at him.

"No, it's okay. This night has been awesome. I want to keep it going. Things didn't go so well last time I hung out with your friends. Maybe it will go better this time." And maybe I'm stalling as well. I wasn't lying when I told Ryder I want to stay at his house, that I want to stay with him. I do. I've known it for a while now, but that doesn't mean I'm not nervous.

"Come on." I put my other shoes on first. We get out of the car, and as soon as we do, I shiver. I forgot my sweater in the Prius; I don't know how since I remembered my shoes. Shows where my mind was. It hasn't really been a big deal all night because we've been inside. I guess I should be thankful this party is at a house.

"I can't believe we're at a party in a suit and dress. I'm going to catch so much shit for this." Ryder nods toward the backside of the house. "I texted Shane. He said they're out back. The house is too crowded and the music is too loud. They have a bonfire going out there."

So much for being inside.

As though I'd spoken that aloud, Ryder glances at my shoulders. "Shit. I didn't even notice you don't have a jacket on." He rolls his eyes and I can tell it's at himself, not me. He thinks he should have noticed earlier.

"Here, wear my jacket."

It's on the tip of my tongue to tell him it's okay, but he's being sweet, and it's cold, and he has long sleeves under it, so I accept his suit jacket. It's big on me but I like that. It smells like Ryder.

He puts his arm around my shoulders and we head to the backyard. He's right, there's a fire back here, a couple of them, actually. They're in barrels. There are kegs and coolers as well.

My heart raps against my chest from nerves and excitement. That's my feeling about this whole night. I want to get to know Ryder's friends better. I can tell how much they mean to him and how much he means to them. I want to go to his house after, but both of those things turn me into Fear again as well.

I'm always someone different, it seems.

I look up at Ryder. "Let's get some beer."

He frowns. "Um…you drink? You told me you didn't. It's not in your plan, remember?"

Neither was he. "Plans can change. Sometimes. As long as it's a good change. Not that drinking is good, but…all kids do it, right? I just want to have fun." And that's partially true. I do just want to have a good time. This is what teenagers do. We experiment.

My hope is this experiment calms my nerves.

"Are you sure? You don't have to, ya know? Not because everyone else is. I'm not drinking. Luke would kick my ass. This is the first time he's let me take his car and I don't want to screw that up."

The little buzz of energy I usually try to ignore starts zipping beneath my skin. I want to do this, I do. And I trust Ryder. He's here, so what could go wrong?

"Let's go." He laughs as I grab his hand and drag him toward one of the kegs. He gets a cup and fills it, shaking his head the whole time.

"Turning bossy again." He hands me the cup with a smile.

"Ryder!" Someone yells and we look over to see his friends in the corner of the yard. Tanner's waving his hand at us.

"Come on." This time I start for them, but Ryder holds me off a minute.

"You don't have to prove yourself."

I fall even more in love with him for that. "I know."

We get to his friends, and everyone says hello. Drea is here with the same guy from the last party. Ryder puts his arm around me and I take a sip of the beer. It's bitter on my tongue and I frown. Gross. Why would people drink this crap?

"That's not what you want to drink. Try this." Drea holds out a cup to me.

Ryder warns, "Dre."

"Screw you, Ryder. I'm trying to be nice. It's not like I'm trying to poison your girlfriend or something." Hurt reflects in her eyes. They're friends, good friends, and I really don't want to come between them.

"It's okay, Ryder." And then I look at Drea. "What is it?"

"It's a Jolly Rancher. Tastes just like the candy." She takes a sip and then offers me the cup. Sweet slides down my throat and I realize I'm definitely not a beer girl. Give me a Jolly Rancher all the way.

"Here, I'll make you one." Drea turns to a little table behind her and starts mixing a drink. I take a drink, and then another. Only half the cup is gone when I get hot all over. Why am I wearing a jacket? It's like a million degrees out here.

Ryder's hands cover mine when I try to take it off. "Ryyyyder. I'm hot!"

"Yeah, you are," some guy says as he walks by.

"Shut the fuck up," Ryder replies, shoving him, and the guy laughs and walks off.

"But I am. Hot, I mean. Not hot, hot. Weather hot. Aren't you hot?" Isn't everyone hot?

"It's been fifteen minutes and you're buzzed already? That's enough of this for you." Ryder tries to take the cup out of my hand but I jerk it back. His friends laugh behind us.

"I'm a big girl. I'm almost eighteen. I know what I'm doing. I won't have anymore than this. You're not the boss of me, Ryder Blackstock."

"I'm not trying to be."

I take a few more swallows and then thread my fingers through his. "Don't be maaaaad."

He sighs and returns my hold. "I'm not. I just don't want you to do something you'll regret."

My cheeks set on fire. He wouldn't say this if any of his other friends were drinking, and yet he's saying it in front of them about me.

In three big gulps, I drink the rest of the alcohol. My skin tingles. My insides tickle, and I'm getting hotter and hotter. "See, I can handle it!" *Shut up. What are you doing?* A voice in the back of my head whispers. I ignore it. Voices mean you're crazy.

"I'll be right back." After turning from Ryder, I don't make it two feet before he steps in front of me..

"Virginia."

"I'm fffffine. I just want to sit by the fire." But I'm hot. Why do I want to sit by the fire?

"I'll go with her." I follow the voice and see Cody.

"Cody! You're here!" Though he's been here the whole time, I think, so I don't know why I said that. "I like you. You're nice to me. You're my favorite out of all Ryder's friends."

He laughs. "I like you, too," as Shane says, "Hey! I'm nice."

"You are. And you have a baby face."

Now it's Shane's turn to laugh. Everyone is laughing except Ryder. Why isn't Ryder laughing?

"Let's go sit," I tell Cody. He glances at Ryder, who nods.

I stumble to an empty chair and Cody sits beside me. Most people are walking around, no one's hanging by the fire. I remember talking a lot with Cody the night Ryder was missing. I really do like him. "Tell me about you and Tanner." Romance has never been my thing, but now it is. I want to gobble up all the love stories I can, maybe since I have one of my own.

I glance at Ryder, who is watching us with a frown. Maybe. "I think Ryder's mad at me."

"Nah, he's worried about you."

"Would Tanner be worried about you?"

"No, but I've been drunk before. Something tells me you haven't."

Ugh. Is it that obvious? "Tanner, tell me about him," I prompt again.

Cody shrugs. "What do you want to know? He's gorgeous, obviously. I was attracted to him when he first came to our school. He was seeing this girl—"

"Wait? A girl?" I'm confused.

"He's bi."

"That's real?"

Cody laughs at me again. He's been doing that a lot. "Of course it's real. Anyway, I thought he was straight at the time, so whatever. One day I was sitting by the fence at lunch. He came over and sat beside me. We talked the whole forty-five minutes and never stopped talking after. We've been together ever since. He broke it off with the girl first, of course."

There's more to it than that. I feel it in my bones. "You're in love with him."

He shrugs. "Of course I am. He's…incredible. Contagious. And he's better than all of us, but he would never see it that way. Kind of like you."

Suddenly, I'm floating. "Really?" Does he really see me like that? The girl who could easily fit in and be a part of them?

"Yeah."

"He loves you just as much as you love him," I tell Cody.

"Yeah…yeah, I know he does. And Ryder loves you. Do you love him?"

I do. My heart flutters. Looking up, I find him. His friends are around him, talking, but Ryder is looking at me. "Yes. He

doesn't make the weight feel as heavy." Even though Cody
doesn't know the conversations Ryder and I have had about the
weight and destiny, I feel like he understands.

Chapter Forty

Ryder

Virginia smiles at Cody. It's a big smile, one of her real ones. Jealousy doesn't settle in my gut. I know there's nothing to be jealous of. Cody's in love with Tanner, and, even if he wasn't, she's a girl. Tanner may bat for both teams, but Cody doesn't.

No, what feels like a heavy weight in my stomach is the thought that I want her over here with me. I want her sober, even though in a lot of ways, she's right. People drink. People our age drink. But there's something that doesn't sit right with her wanting to do it tonight. I think she's doing it because of me, and that thought won't stop shooting through my body with each pump of my heart.

Cody stands and holds his hand out to her. He helps her up and then follows as she walks my way. Each step she takes my heart goes faster, and I wonder what the hell happened to me. How falling for someone can make me feel things I didn't know existed, and how I'm okay with that.

Virginia's arms wrap around my neck and she buries her face in my chest. "Cody says you love meeee."

Yeah, she is totally wasted. "Cody's a smart guy." I nod thanks at him, before he goes over to Tanner. "And you're drunk."

She mumbles something. I wrap my arms around her before I look up. Shane smiles at me, and then takes a hit of his pipe. He's been sucking on that thing too much. I glance at Drea; she's sitting on the ground, staring at it.

In a lot of ways, I've always been trapped by my life, only I didn't realize it. Now, I'm trapped in a different way—between the girl in my arms and hurting my friend. There's no way to stop the hurt without losing Virginia. Maybe it makes me weak, but I tackle the Shane thing instead because it's easier. "Gimme your pipe."

"Huh?" he replies.

"Give it to me. You're smoking too much. Your eyes are redder than the fire."

He rolls them at me but hands it over, and a baggie, which I stick into my pocket.

"Look at you, being all responsible now."

"Asshole," I tease him.

Words vibrate against my chest. "I need to pee."

"That's what happens when you down a cup of alcohol like it's nothing. Come on. I'll take you to find a bathroom."

The house is so packed full of people, it's hard to get through. I want out of the place. Want to take Virginia home, even if it's not to mine. She doesn't belong here.

Once we find the bathroom, she goes in and I wait outside the door for her. My brain is cluttered with all these thoughts and I can't seem to push them the hell out. I can't figure out why Virginia wanted to get drunk tonight. If it's because she thinks that's what I want, or if I'm a bad influence on her. It just doesn't add up.

A few minutes later, she comes out smiling. *Let's get outta here…* Instead of saying that, I lead her back the way we came. She wanted to be here with my friends tonight, and I want her to have a good time. But then we step outside, and I can't stop myself from turning to her and saying, "Hey. Why'd you want to drink? There's nothing wrong with it, but I want to know. And why did you get pissed at me and leave with Cody?"

She looks down, but with a finger under her chin, I tilt her head back upward.

"It's just me. I showed you my scars; you can tell me anything."

Her eyes get glassy, pool with unshed tears. I lean against the house, away from everyone, taking her with me.

"I'm sorry. I screwed up the whole night. I wasn't mad at you… I was scared. I told you I want to go back to your house, and I *do* want to go, but then I got freaked because it's big… Really big. I didn't even want to date in high school, and now I'm with you, and—"

"Hey, I don't expect anything from you. I don't want you to do anything you don't want to do. It's…you make me…"

"COPS!" someone yells from the front of the house.

My heart drops to my feet.

Virginia's eyes go wide.

I have to get her out of here. "Come on, Virginia, let's go." There is no way she's going to pass a breathalyzer. Fuck. I'm going to get her in trouble. This girl who needs order and stability, and I'm going to screw it up for her.

Grabbing her hand, I run. She stumbles a little. I'm sure it's hard to run in her tight dress, but thankfully it's short. "Come on, boss lady. You got this. Let's go." We climb the fence. I drop to the other side and then reach for her, helping her over. People are yelling, running, bodies everywhere. I don't know where my friends are right now, I just have to hope they can get themselves out of here.

"It'll be okay. I promise. I won't let you get caught." Our hands are latched again and I start running with her. It's dark as hell out. We're in the woods behind the house. Part of me thinks this is a terrible idea because we could get lost, but I can't risk her getting caught, either.

Voices are everywhere. The stomp of feet. Sporadic bursts of light as though someone is running with flashlights. I highly doubt anyone at the party had a flashlight with them.

My chest burns from how far and fast we run. I know Virginia has to be feeling the same. And she's in a dress. At least she changed her shoes.

"Ryder… I'm…scared. My…dad…will…freak." She can hardly speak, we're running so hard.

"It's cool. I'll find us a place to hide. We'll be okay." I told her I would take care of her, and I will.

I almost trip a dozen times. Finally, I find this little wall of rocks, hidden by a bunch of trees. I duck behind them with Virginia as she struggles to catch her breath.

"Oh my God. Dad. Mom. School. What if Stanford finds out? Can I lose my scholarship? This was stupid. Why did I do this? It was reckless…reckless. It was Mom."

She's rocking back and forth. I don't know what most of what she just said means, but I hear the panic in her voice. It punches my heart over and over. "You'll be okay. We're good," I whisper. It's quiet, no one else around us. I don't know what

226

way everyone went or who got caught.

And then I see lights far away, and coming closer. Hear voices that I know don't belong to anyone who was drinking at that party. Virginia gasps. Squeezes my hand.

"Who's out there!" a cop yells. "Come out, hands where we can see them."

We're fucked. No, I am.

"Here." I shove my phone into her hand. "The second we're gone, you call Shane. He'll come get you. He'll find you. If he doesn't answer the first time, call Tanner or Cody. If they don't, call Luke. They'll find you, I promise."

I would trust any of them with my life...even my brother. My brother, who is going to kill me.

"What? No!" She shakes her head.

The voices get closer. "You're going to get caught if I don't. It's not a big deal. I haven't even been drinking. I promise."

I press a quick kiss to her lips. "Call them the second we're gone. Don't screw around. All their numbers are there."

"Ryder!" she whispers, but I ignore her. I stand up and walk away.

"Here, piggy, piggy!" I yell as I run toward the police. It isn't long before they're surrounding me, searching me, locking handcuffs on my wrists.

And then they take me away.

But they don't go out and find Virginia.

Chapter Forty-One

Virginia

Shane answers on the first ring. "You guys make it out, man?"

"It's me, Lulu—I mean, Virginia. We had to run, and then Ryder got caught. He gave me his phone and said to call you."

Shane curses. "Where are you?"

From then on out, it's as though I'm watching or listening to everything happen. I tell them the woods, but I don't know where. They're out here, too, and we get off the phone and they call it until they find me. It takes an hour. The whole time I'm thinking about Ryder, angry at myself for letting him go; but it happened so fast, I was so scared I just didn't know what to do.

Cody reaches me first. I let him hug me and try not to cry on him. It's hard because he feels like a friend.

He's the one who drives when we get to Shane's car, because he's the only one who is completely sober.

"I can't believe he parked his car at the party. He's usually smarter than that."

Shane hadn't parked right by the house.

Everyone is talking and trying to figure out what to do. It's making my head hurt, my vision go blurry. I just want to get to Ryder and make sure he's safe.

"How did he get caught?" Tanner asks.

"It was so fast. We were hiding and they were closing in on us. He just gave me his phone, told me to call Shane, and ran toward them."

"And you let him go?!" Drea yells. "What the hell?"

My eyes pinch closed, as though that will change everything. "You think I don't know it was stupid? I was scared. I've never done something like this before, and I'd been drinking. I wasn't thinking! It all happened so fast and—"

"Exactly the reason you don't need to hang out with us," Drea spats.

"Dre, lay off her," Shane says as Cody asks, "Where am I going, guys? To get Luke?"

"Of course you take her side," Drea counters.

It's all getting louder and louder. A chalkboard inside my head with a thousand nails scratching it. *There once was a girl named Fear...Weak...Reckless...*

"Are you kidding me right now? I always have your back, Dre. Always."

Tanner jumps in before she can reply to Shane. "Can you guys save this for later? It's just making things worse."

The car gets silent as though everyone knows Shane is about to drop a bomb. "Shit! He had my weed on him! Do you know if he remembered to dump it?"

My heart tries to climb up my throat. I drop my head against the seat, my silence saying everything.

"Luke is going to kill him. He's been arrested twice..." Shane states what we already know.

And it's my fault. Why did I let him go? Why did I drink? If I hadn't, none of this would have happened. My stupid decision got Ryder in trouble. This isn't me. I'm not supposed to make rash, irresponsible decisions like this.

"Take me home," tumbles out of my mouth.

"Are you kidding me? Ryder gets arrested for you and you want us to take you home?" Drea shouts.

"Shut up! I know you don't like me, but you're not helping anything! Take me home, Cody. Now. My dad, he's a lawyer. He'll help."

It doesn't matter that I'll get in trouble, that he won't trust me. What matters is Ryder.

Cody curses, but it's Shane who says, "Ryder is going to kick my ass for this. Let's go to her house, Cody."

It takes close to ten years to get home. The second Cody pulls up in the driveway I'm out of the car and running for my house. "Dad!" I yell as soon as I get inside.

"Daddy!" I scream again as I take the stairs. Dad's jumping out of bed by the time I push his door open.

"Lulu? What's wrong?" His voice is higher pitched and faster paced than usual. "Are you okay?"

I can only imagine how I look. There's dirt all over me, my dress is ripped and my hair a mess. "Yes, but it's Ryder. I need your help. Please, I need you to help him."

He learns almost everything right then, standing in the middle of his bedroom in the dim light of his lamp.

Dad sits on the bed, not looking at me. "Let me get this

straight, Lulu. You not only lied to me about where you were staying tonight and about having a date to the dance, but you've also been lying for weeks. You're dating a boy from another town who we know nothing about. You went to a party tonight, got drunk, and now you want me to go and help the boy who got you to lie about everything? Oh, and who also might have had drugs on him?"

Before he even finished, my head was already shaking. "It wasn't his, and he didn't get me to lie. He didn't know I told you I was going to Jamie's. He wanted to meet you." When Dad's eyes meet mine, it's me who turns away, unable to hold his stare. "It was my choice. I know you're not judgmental, but I was scared…scared if you met him, you wouldn't let me see him."

"That's not selling me on him, Lulu."

"But it wasn't his fault! Ryder didn't want me to drink in the first place. He sacrificed himself for me. He ran to the cops so I wouldn't be in trouble for being drunk. I shouldn't have let him because he's been arrested before and—"

"He's been arrested before?" Dad pushes to his feet. "This keeps getting better and better!"

It's then I realize I messed up even worse. Dad isn't going to help him, and he's not going to let me see Ryder anymore, either. "Please." I go to him. Hug him. "I'm sorry I lied, so sorry, but it's not Ryder's fault. He's made some mistakes, but he's had a hard life, and he wants to be better. He's *trying* to be better. He knew he would get into more trouble than I would tonight, but he did it for me. You're the one who told me people make mistakes, that they deserve second chances. You're the one who said what matters is the kind of person someone is, and he's a *good* guy. He was raised badly, but he and his brother are trying to overcome it. He…I don't feel so alone when I'm with him."

Dad sucks in a deep breath. "Why do you feel alone?"

"I don't know…"

And now he's holding me tighter. His nightshirt is wet from my tears. I don't know how long we stay there before Dad speaks. "I can't make you any promises. I'm not sure there's much I can do anyway. It's probably a pretty cut and dry charge, but I'll make some calls and go see what information I can get; but you're not getting off easy here, Lulu. We're going to have a big talk about what's going on with you. Your mother and I will have to decide how we feel about you seeing this boy, and…you're not going to be able to avoid your mom anymore. I want you to spend a weekend with her, maybe more than one weekend. It's time you start acting like an adult."

A weekend with my mom. Amelia. Mom. Even worse than that, I might not be able to see him again. My chest caves in the weight is so heavy.

But Dad will help Ryder, that's what matters. "Okay, whatever you want. I'll do it."

Chapter Forty-Two

Ryder

Virginia's dad sits across the table from me at the juvenile detention center. Her *dad*. My hands shake, the bad kind again, but now I'm wondering if they're all bad.

"It wasn't her fault, sir. It was a party with my friends. I'm the one who wanted to go."

"That's funny, because she said the same thing about you." He pushes his glasses up his nose. "The main charge is trespassing. The owner of the home didn't know the party was taking place there. We could try and say you hadn't been there since they didn't find you on the property, but your brother's car was found there. You had a pipe and marijuana in your possession. It was less than an ounce, which is good, but with your record, trespassing, and all things considered, I'm positive they would get a conviction.

"I got them to give you community service and probation if you plead guilty. You can choose to go to court, but remember, this is your third offense. We're lucky they're overworked and the homeowner isn't pushing it, otherwise this offer wouldn't even be on the table. If I hadn't been here tonight, I doubt they would have even offered it."

Luke sighs from next to me.

"Yeah...yeah, okay. I'll do that." If it keeps her out of trouble and her dad off her back, it's worth it. It's not like what they said isn't true anyway. I did all the things Mr. Nichols said.

And she went to him...she went to him to help me. Who does shit like that? Her dad trusted her; pretty much gave her free reign, and now that's going to end. Plus, now he knows she's with me. Virginia did that for *me*.

It's the first time someone other than my friends, didn't just bail on me.

"I'll be right back, then." Her dad stands and walks out of the room. The second he does, Luke spits fire at me.

"What the hell were you thinking, Ryder? You took her to a party? You went to get high when you *knew* you had my car with you and that you needed to drive? You got Virginia drunk?"

"Yep." I lean back in my chair and cross my arms.

I could tell him that I would have rather taken Virginia home that night than go to the party.

I could tell him I didn't want her to drink.

That I stayed sober myself, and the weed hadn't been mine.

That I know I fucked up, and I would do anything to take it back. I don't want to be the guy who has to run with Virginia through the woods so she doesn't get arrested.

I want to be *more*.

But it doesn't matter anyway, so I say none of it. If there's one thing I've learned, it's that the only thing that matters in life is what you do, not what you wanted to do.

"Jesus, Ry, I trusted you. I had to pay to get my car out of impound. We're lucky Virginia's dad is helping you at all—"

"Lucky? I don't want his fucking help, man. The only reason I'm taking it is because of her. I would rather he didn't know all this shit!" Him knowing makes it more real. The truth is, she would have never gone to a party like that if it wasn't for me. She never would have gotten drunk and almost arrested, either. It doesn't matter if I wanted to go to that party or not, it's still my fault.

"Just leave it alone, Luke. I'll get a job and pay you back for the dance and your car. We can go back to you not trusting me, to make it easier on both of us."

This time he doesn't tell me he'd rather I not work and focus on school. My brother just sits in the chair and pretends I didn't speak to him.

We both do that until Virginia's dad comes back in. He has paperwork to sign, which I do. Luke makes it out the door before I stop. "Just a sec, man." Not giving my brother a chance to reply, I close the door—him on the outside, me on the inside.

"I just…" I push my hands into my pockets. "She wouldn't have been there if it wasn't for me."

Her dad leans against the table. "I know that, which is why I'm going to ask you not to see her again for a while. I'm not stupid. She's almost eighteen, and I know there's really nothing I can do to stop her, but Lulu is going through a lot. She might not realize it—hell, I'm not even sure I realized it—but she is, and it's only going to get worse. My daughter has always had a good head on her shoulders. Kids make mistakes, I get that, but it's also my job to protect her to the best of my ability, and at this point, I'm not sure approving of your relationship with her is doing that."

His words cement everything I've always known, show me my destiny carved into the walls of ancient pyramids that have been around for thousands of years.

Just like Dad always knew, and just like Luke did, too, I'm built to be at the opposite end of the scale from people like Virginia and even my brother. The one that keeps the balance between people like them who will do good things and people like me who won't.

I close my eyes, wondering if the hole in my chest will do me in; take me over until there's nothing left but darkness. "Yes, sir."

Once facing the door again, I twist the knob, squeeze it with all the strength I have in my hand. "You're right about it just being a mistake. Virginia is a good person...the best. Maybe it doesn't matter, but she was always cool to me, even when most people wouldn't have been. Virginia almost made me feel like I could do it."

"Does she let you call her Virginia?" he asks.

"Yeah." I don't tell him Lulu isn't a strong enough name for her, but it's not. She'll always be Virginia to me.

The door is open when he asks, "Made you feel like you could do what?"

"Be a better man."

Chapter Forty-Three

Virginia

There once was a girl named Sadness. She lived and breathed her name. It became every part of her. Her name lived in every cell of her body, every particle in her blood. It danced on beats of her heart, taunting her. Echoed in her head, reminding her of the person she was.

Sadness didn't know how to swim, not from the depths of her tears. They got bigger and bigger, deeper and deeper, until her head sunk below the surface, the rocks in her pockets making it impossible to stay afloat.

Sadness was even sadder down here.

She tried and tried to take the rocks from her pockets, but Sadness had glued them there.

One rock for the boy she lost, and not just because she lost him, either. Because she didn't want him to blame himself.

Another rock for the father she loved more than anything, the man who was always there for her, but who now didn't trust her.

A rock for her mom, who she loved, but was scared to love at the same time.

There was another rock for her own mistakes, and another for her fear. Her decisions and the pain Sadness had inflicted on everyone she loved.

The weight she carried couldn't be carried. There was nothing left to do, besides live in her tears.

~*~

"Shut up!" I sit in the middle of my bed, with my knees up, fingers tightly woven in my hair as I rock back and forth. "Just shut up!"

I want the words gone, the stories that fill my head. They don't belong there, and yet more and more I'm drowning in them. They want out, to be free. Mom once told me that writing *is* freeing, but to me it's chains—chains, ropes, and handcuffs, telling me who I'm going to be.

Is that how it started for Mom? Voices in her head that wanted to escape? They came out in stories and books, and other people? Even to my own ears that sounds stupid. I'm a smart girl, but I think the heart really is the strongest muscle in the body. It can bench press a million times more weight than your brain, because no matter how much my head tells me something, my heart always overpowers it out. My heart, the little house in my chest where all the parts of me live, all the bits and pieces that make me —The fear and loathing, the loneliness and sadness.

The walls are strong; the brick house that keeps out the wolf, even when I know this is a wolf I should let in. My brain.

"Lulu? Are you about ready to go?" Dad calls through my door before pushing it open.

I don't reply.

"It's been two weeks. Don't you think it's about time you

started talking to me?"

Something sharp on the handle of my suitcase pokes my hand when I grab it.

Dad sighs. "If you're going to beat traffic, you need to head to your mom's now."

Without a word to him, I walk out of my room.

Chapter Forty-Four

Ryder

Cool air rushes in from outside when I open the door for my friends.

"Are you sure you don't want to go out? You only turn eighteen once." Tanner asks.

"Nah, I'm cool. Thanks, man."

He frowns but nods and then walks out. Cody sets a hand on my shoulder and squeezes before he bails, too.

"Ry…"

"Don't. We're good," I tell Drea. I see the worry in her eyes. The apology. "If you start feeling bad for me then I know I'm really fucked. I just feel like chilling today." Like Cody did on my shoulder, Drea squeezes my hand and walks out.

"I'll catch you guys in a minute." Shane closes the door. "Where's Luke?" My best friend walks over to the window and looks out.

I go over and stand beside him. Even though Shane already

knows the answer to his question, I say, "Work. He has to take extra shifts to cover all the money I cost him."

Shane fingers the wheel on his skateboard, quiet. It's got to be a full minute before he speaks. "You ever feel like you're stuck in like...what the fuck are they? One of those wheels hamsters run in? Over and over, you keep going, but you're not getting anywhere?"

A sarcastic laugh falls out of my mouth. "Yeah, I get that."

"I know you do."

More quiet, which is strange. Shane either doesn't say anything or he cuts to the chase. This isn't like him. "I'm sorry, man. About you and Virginia. If I would've been with you, I would have taken the hit so you didn't have to. Then at least you could still see her."

And he would have. I'd do the same for him. "It was only a matter of time, anyway. Thanks, though. You'll always be my boy."

Shane laughs. "Now we sound like Tanner and Cody."

I chuckle and then wait for him to say what he wants to say.

"I get it, though...being into someone when you know it will never fucking happen."

My neck gets a sharp pain, I whip my head in his direction so quickly. "What? Who?" Shane never hooks up with anyone.

Slowly, he glances up. For a split second I think he's going to say me and I wonder how in the hell I missed *that,* but then he turns his head towards the window and looks out.

Whoa. "Dre?" And then, holy shit. "Why didn't you tell me?"

More playing with the wheel on his board. "Because she's always been into you. I thought you'd end up falling for her. You guys messed around enough." He shakes his head and looks down. "Wanted you to be happy."

Guilt eats through my gut. "Fuck, Shane. You should have told me. I never would have touched her."

Two people. I hurt not just one but *two* of the people who are the most important to me—Shane and Drea both. And that's not counting my brother or Virginia.

"So you're not…"

"No. Hell no." He thinks I'm going to start hooking up with Drea again because it's over with Virginia. "It's not like that. I really love her. Virginia. And even if I didn't, I wouldn't do that again. I wouldn't hurt Dre…or you."

He thinks about this a minute, then nods. "Okay, I'm gonna bounce. You sure you don't want to come out?"

"No. I'm good."

Shane goes out to his car, and I watch my friends drive away. It's a couple hours later as I'm sitting on my bed when I hear the sound outside my window.

My room faces the back, away from the street, and the only thing I can think is that Virginia came to see me. There's no one else who would come to my window. Maybe she's freaked thinking Luke is here.

When I pull the blinds and see who it is, my first thought is disappointment that it's not her. My second thought is *holy shit…*

My stupid hand shakes again as I reach for the latch on the window. "Dad?"

"Is Luke here?" he asks. He's grown a beard since I last saw him. Not a thick one, but it's different. His hair used to be dark like mine, but now it has an auburn tint to it as if he dyed it.

"No." Dad's here. I can't believe he's here. My body is unable to move.

"Come outside with me. I don't have long."

I physically have to force myself to move, though I'm not sure why. Shock or fear? Or is it something worse? For years all I thought about was the day my dad would come and take me away, let me *live* again. Someone who knows who I am, and is proud of that person. Now, he's here, and what I really want to do is run.

"You didn't think I'd miss your eighteenth birthday, did you?" Dad pulls me into a hug the minute I step out back. His arms feel different. He's wearing gloves where the fingers stick through, which strikes me as weird, even though I can't pinpoint why.

Yes...you've missed quite a few of my birthdays since you left slams into my head, followed by, *it's not his fault.* It's not as if Dad ever wanted to leave me...and he came back. Like I always knew he would, he came back. For me. Not because he had to, because he wanted to. Dad looks around before focusing on me again.

"Listen, Ry. I don't have a lot of time. I'm jumpy just being in this piece of shit town again. I hated leaving you with Luke, but I didn't have a choice. They would have looked a lot harder if I had a minor with me. You're eighteen now, though. You can leave and no one can do shit about it. I have this really great gig back east. We're staying outside Detroit. Jesus, it's cold as a witch's tit out there. You'll get used to it. Anyway, we're taking cars. We need a follow driver. I know it's not the best gig, but it's a start, and you'll work your way up real quick and the money is great."

"You came back," sort of falls out of my mouth. Michigan. He's been in Michigan.

"Of course I did. I told you I'd come back for you. Is that brother of yours filling your head with shit about me?"

I shake my head.

"Good. Now listen, I told the new crew how good you are—how you were fucking born to lift shit. You prove yourself as a follow driver, and you'll be able to move up. You won't believe the money we're making down there, kid."

Dad shoves an envelope into my hand. "I got you a bus ticket and a fake ID, in case you don't have one. I don't want anyone to be able to trace where you went. If you have a car, you can't take it, but it's not like we can't get you one when you get to Detroit."

My head is spinning, going out of control. "What about school?"

Dad's forehead wrinkles. "Fuck school, Ryder. What the hell is a high school diploma going to do for you? Teach you to live? Survive? Since when did school matter to you? He did this, didn't he?" Dad steps backward. "Luke turned you against me."

"No!" I shake my head. "He didn't."

Dad smiles. "Good. It would be a waste, losing skills like yours. The ticket is for Monday. There's the name of a hotel in the envelope, too. When you get to Detroit, go there. Stay a few days, and then when I'm sure everything's cool, I'll come get you."

Dad turns and heads for the trees behind our house before he stops, looks at me, and winks. "It's good to see ya, kid. I'm proud of you for never turning your back on me."

He disappears and my head pounds with an overload of every emotion.

I'm proud of you.

I told you I'd come back for you.

I told the new crew how good you are.

I hated leaving you.

Luke never wanted me.

There's never really been anything I'm good at besides working with Dad.

I lost Virginia. Hurt Drea and Shane, and made things uncomfortable with our friendship.

Now Dad is back. He wants me—*needs* me. With him, I don't have to feel guilty for my past. There's no judgment. No complicated drama. Just my destiny waiting for me.

The choice is already made.

Chapter Forty-Five

Virginia

"Do you want to watch a movie or something?" Mom asks on the second night of our "bonding" weekend.

"Whatever." I'm being a brat, I know. It's been the same with Dad, but I can't seem to stop myself. It's different with Mom. There are more words, but words don't always mean more is being said. It doesn't mean we're closer than Dad and I, or that we've made some kind of breakthrough.

I think it might mean I missed her even more than I realized, though.

"You know what? I changed my mind. We're not going to watch a movie." Mom turns off the TV. "We're going to talk. I want you to start journaling. We've talked about this before, but I mean it this time. Dad and I spoke. Whatever it is you have going on, whatever you're feeling, you're not getting it out, and that's important, Virginia. You have to get it out. If you won't talk to us, then writing—"

"I talked to Ryder! But then, he lives in the wrong town so you won't let me see him." Every word that just came out of my mouth is a lie. Yes, I talked to Ryder, but not completely. I never told him everything. And I know my parents. The fact that Ryder is poor and lives where he does has nothing to do with their decision. Still, I don't take back the words.

"That's not fair. You know that's not the way it is."

"Life's not fair." I toss back a statement I've heard a hundred times over the years.

Mom sighs and sits up farther on the couch. Her body language changes, gets more wooden, determined. "You're acting like a child right now, and I think you know it. You're almost eighteen years old. You want to prove you can handle a relationship with that boy, and that you'll make good decisions, then you need to act like it. And if you don't want to write, that's fine. You'll talk to someone, then. I refuse to sit back and let you keep things bottled in, because one day, that bottle will explode."

My legs jerk, bounce me off the couch. "*Talk* to someone?" A shrink. She thinks I need a shrink? Oh, God.

Mom pushes to her feet, too. "Yes! If that's what it takes! I am not going to lose you. I'm not going to lose our relationship. I'm not going to let you lose yourself. We'll see someone together if you want, or you can go alone, but you need to get this out, Virginia. Your anger and hurt toward me, I get it, but you have to let it out, and you're not doing that. It's going to eat you alive."

"Maybe it already has!" I shove away from the couch to look for my shoes. "You don't get it. You don't know what it's like."

"Then tell me." Mom follows behind me.

I can't. So I don't answer.

"If you can't tell me, you're going to tell someone else. I made you an appointment. Her name is—"

I let loose a scream of frustration. How dare she make decisions like this without talking to me? She's deciding who I am, what I need, when she doesn't know anything. When she's still trying to figure herself out.

There once was a girl named...

"Mommy?"... "Ugh, it's you again."

"You'll be just like her, you know. You try to hide it, try to deny it, but I see it in you. Every day I look in the mirror at your mom's eyes, and I see the same look flash back. The one you're showing me right now. You want it, don't you, Lulu, or Virginia, or whatever your name is? You want to run free, like her. You want to be wild and fun, and that's what scares you. You know you're already her..."

No... I shake my head. "I'm not you! I'll never be you! I don't need to talk to a shrink because I'm not crazy!" Tears are pouring down my face.

My head is full of a voice that's not mine. A voice that's my mom's, only it isn't her speaking. Or maybe it is. I don't know. Maybe Samantha said all the things Mom has wanted to say to me over the years. Maybe she knows more than I do. Maybe she's right...

She told me I'm Mom. She sees the same look in my eyes that she sees in the mirror. My whole life I've feared she's right. "I'm not crazy," I repeat. "I'm not you."

Mom stops moving. Her eyes are closed, her body curved in defeat. And then it's like someone puts new bones into her body. She stands straight. Her arms get stiff. Her legs almost look like they lengthen. When her eyes open, I know it's not my mom I'm looking at.

There is no way to describe how that feels. People on the outside, they don't get it. They don't see. People don't believe in DID, but it's real. I've lived it, and if you haven't, you can't know.

"Now you've done it," someone whom I assume is Amelia says.

"D-done what?" I take a step backward. *Mom...I'm sorry.*

"Why are you backing away? I'm not going to hurt her. Don't you get it? I'm here to protect her. We always have been."

"Protect her?" My voice is soft. "Protect her from what?"

"From pain...from remembering. We're not supposed to tell you. She wouldn't want you to know. You're a smart girl, Virginia. Don't tell me you haven't done your research." Amelia goes to the chair beside me and sits down. And I want her back. I want my mom back. I want us to be okay, be normal. Whatever it takes.

"It's easier to pretend someone like me couldn't exist inside someone else if you don't actually know anything about it. Sometimes when the mind goes through so much hurt, so much pain, the only way to deal with it is for someone else to do it for you. That's where I come in. As much as you hated Samantha, that's where she came in as well. We deal with the memories your mom can't handle, the ones she sees every time she closes her eyes."

Oh God. What is she talking about? What happened to Mom? *Oh God, oh God, oh God.*

"Your grandma's boyfriend was the first to hurt her. Over and over for years. That's why Annette left. She couldn't handle what she let happen."

"No!" I close my hands over my ears. "No, no, no, no, no!"

"Yes!" Amelia screams. "Yes, and it didn't end there. She was on the streets afterward. For years. You'll never know what she's lived through, the things she had to do to survive. *She* may never know it all, but you're the one she wants to protect from it.

You're the one she allows to hurt her, because she knows it would hurt you to know."

"Oh God." I stumble backward, and fall to the floor. My chest screams at me, aches in pain. My body, it's like it's not there. I can't feel anything except the pain in my heart. My chest heaves with strangled breaths. Someone hurt her; hurt her bad enough that her mind created other people to deal with it.

And I've hated her for it. Punished her by withholding myself from her. Didn't take the time to look into her disorder because I wanted to pretend it didn't exist—because it was easier on me.

"I can't…I don't know…" What to say or how to feel. I haven't stood up but I'm still moving backward, scooting backward as though getting farther away will mean none of this is true.

"I'm sorry," Amelia whispers.

It's then I realize I'm not any of the people I thought I was. I'm not Perfect, Fear, or Destiny. I am a girl named Hate, and I hate myself for what I've done. For hurting her. For trying to turn Mom into hate as well.

"I have to go."

Chapter Forty-Six

Ryder

One bag. Most of my stuff fits in one bag. My clothes, anyway. It's not that I'll need much else. I have stuff to wear to get me through until Monday, and then everything else is in the bag sitting in the middle of my floor right now.

In a day and a half, I'll be out of here. Out of Luke's hair so he can live his life.

I'll be away from Virginia... Instead of a body, I feel like I'm a shell. Like someone emptied me, hollowed me out.

"Dude, chill the hell out. You're being an idiot," I tell myself. This has always been my plan, being with Dad. There's no reason to freak out about it now.

But that was before Virginia. Before I realized this isn't who I want to be. Now, I just don't know if I have a choice.

There's a pounding at my front door. I almost ignore it, not in the mood to hang out with my friends, but stand up instead. They deserve to know what's going on.

The pounding gets louder.

"Chill out! I'm coming."

There's a little whimper through the thin door, and I know it's not Shane on the other side. I run.

"Virginia?" I open the door, and as soon as I do, she's in my arms. Squeezing my neck and my hand is in her hair and she feels so...so right that I don't want to let her go. Ever. "What are you doing here? You're not supposed to see me."

And then she's crying and my heart is racing and I'm holding her tighter. "Hey, what's wrong?"

"I'm sorry... I didn't know where else to go."

"Don't be sorry. I'm here. You can always come to me. I'm here." Maybe that's another thing I'm good at...being there for someone. I would never walk away from her when she needs me. I wouldn't from my friends, either.

She cries harder and I pick her up. Her body is so limp, she goes easily into my arms. Her arms wrap around my neck and I'm holding behind her back and under her knees as I walk into my room.

I lay her on the bed and try to move away, but Virginia's hand is wrapped up tightly in the hoodie she gave me as she holds me close.

So I lay down with her. I wrap my arm under her, letting Virginia's head rest on my chest. I hold her, hoping to find the right words to say. Hoping to find a way to make it better.

Chapter Forty-Seven
Virginia

"It wasn't her fault," I whisper against Ryder's cheek.

"What wasn't?"

"Everything." A deep breath fills my lungs. I exhale. And tell Ryder everything: What DID is—Dissociative Identity Disorder—about Samantha, Robin and Amelia. About things that they've said to me and how I felt. I tell him about the stories locked inside my head that I've been scared to let free. My fear of being like her. Samantha's promise that I already am. He learns about the times I've been rejected by her, how much I thought she must hate me if Samantha did. The times I've wanted to be like Mom or do something crazy like Mom does, and how that scares me more than anything.

"That first night...on the dock. I think that's what the night was about."

He holds me tighter and lets me speak.

When it becomes too much and I sit up, he does too. He leans against the wall, and then it's too hard to look at him so I lay on my side, facing away from Ryder with my head in his lap instead.

"I feel like there are so many different people inside me, I don't know who I am. I try to be Lulu the girl who is responsible and gets good grades. Who is never late and who does well at FBLA. What if that's not who I am? What if I'm all these other people I try not to be?"

He strokes my hair and I close my eyes. They hurt from crying and lack of sleep.

"You're not," he whispers.

Maybe not, but I'm not a good person, either. "It wasn't her fault, Ryder. If I would have looked into it, maybe I would have known. Maybe I could have helped. But I was too angry to do it. People hurt her and I hated her for it. I tried to do everything in my power not to be like her, when I should have loved her and been there for her. I hurt her, too…"

I thought all my tears were gone but they start again, running down my face as though something is after them. He keeps running his fingers through my hair.

"You didn't know. No one can blame you for that, but you know now. You'll do the right thing. That's who you are, Virginia. You're the best person I know."

I want that to be true. I want to do the right thing, want to be as strong as Mom. Because she is. I see that now. *She's* the strongest person I know.

Chapter Forty-Eight

Ryder

My hand doesn't stop moving in Virginia's hair until she falls asleep. Gently, I lift her head out of my lap. She doesn't stir, even when I gently pull her cell out of her pocket, hoping like crazy I'm doing the right thing.

Luke is sitting on the couch. His mouth opens the second I walk in, but I hold up a hand. "Don't. It's not what you think." I have no doubt he saw Virginia's car out front and wants to give me shit for it.

I close my eyes, pull in a deep breath and then let it out. When I open them again, I look up her dad's number in her phone and hit call.

Please let this be the right thing. I don't want to betray her.

"Lulu? Where are you?" he answers.

"It's me...Um... Ryder. Virginia is sleeping. She came to my house a couple hours ago. She's pretty upset, and I could tell something major went down, but I didn't want you to worry. I want you to know she's okay."

NYRAE DAWN

"We'll come and get her—"

"No. I mean, don't. Please. Look," back and forth, I pace the room. "I know you're not real fond of me. I know you think she can do better, but that's not what this is about. She's...she's having a hard time. She's feeling awful, and she's angry at herself. She cried herself to sleep. I didn't even...I didn't tell her I was calling."

My stomach rolls over and I feel the need to keep talking.

"Like I said, I don't want you to worry, but I think it's a bad idea to come and get her. She needs to work through this a little, and she needs some sleep. I'll talk to her about going home tomorrow, and I'll sleep in the living room and everything. You can talk to Luke..." I look at my brother and see something shining back at me I've rarely seen before. Respect.

Luke nods, still watching me like he has no idea who I am. Maybe he doesn't. Maybe I don't.

"Please, just let her breathe a little. I just want what's best for her."

The line is so quiet, I almost think he hung up. It's his sudden breathing that let's me know he's even there. "Thank you for calling me, Ryder. You didn't have to. That's a real mature thing for you to do. Please, if you can tell her to come home in the morning, her mother and I are here waiting for her."

The second I hang up the phone, Luke's hand is on my shoulder. "Holy shit, Ry. You're such a good guy. Do you know that?"

I roll my eyes and step out of his hold. "You wouldn't say that if you knew that Dad was here."

"What?"

My knee pops once as I walk over to the couch and sit down.

"He's stealing cars and he wants me in on it. I have a bus ticket in my pocket and a packed bag in my room. Still think I'm a good guy?"

Luke's jaw tenses up…and then he walks over to the couch and sits beside me. "Yeah, I do. He tried to make it otherwise, but it didn't work. Dad never would have called Virginia's family just then. Jesus," Luke's hands fist. "I am so pissed at him. You were just a kid, and he took you under his wing, glamorizing his lifestyle when he knew how much you loved him. He took advantage of you, Ryder. He was the adult. He should have known better. You were a kid who loved his dad, and he tried to turn you into another version of himself. I will always hate him for that. I'll hate myself for it, too, because I'm your brother. I should have protected you."

My body goes rigid as I try to figure out if I really just heard what I think I did.

"God, you are so smart. And you're always so loving. I think that's why it made it easier for him to get to you. Your heart was always bigger than both mine or his, and I let him prey on that. I left you with him." Luke swings his arm to the side, knocking everything off the table. "I was so damn selfish when I left you with him. I told myself that I could fix everything in time. That I'd show you that you could get out of here. That I could make something with my life so that when you turned eighteen, I could have you come live with me, maybe help you through school. But none of that changes the fact that I left you with him."

Luke tries to shove to his feet but I jerk my hand up, grabbing his arm. I'm squeezing it. I feel the pressure but I can't seem to let go. "You thought I was smart…? You were going to come back for me…?"

Luke sits back down, turns to look at me. "Always, Ryder. When I realized he was grooming you to be like him, that's all I could think about. Getting out, going to school, and then getting you. I always wanted to come back for you. You loved him so much; you would have done anything for him. You're the same way with Shane, Drea, Cody and Tanner. You're the same with Virginia. I always knew you had it in you to be the best of us all."

Logically, I know I've cried before. Everyone has. But I don't remember a time, not one single time, that I've cried. Until now. As long as I can remember, I've looked up to my brother. I thought he could do anything...and I thought he hated me so I denied how I felt about him. But he didn't. He wanted to make a better life for me. He wanted to come back for me. He's been working his ass off for *me*. "I thought you couldn't wait to get away from me."

And then Luke is hugging me, and I swear to God, I think he's crying, too. I hug him back and hear what he said about who I am, and there has never been a person I wanted to be more than who Luke said I am.

"I know I told Virginia's dad I'll sleep out here, but I don't want her to wake up alone. We'll sleep with the door open, and I'll pass out on the floor, but I can't leave her."

He nods. "Okay. I trust you."

"Thanks, Luke...for everything."

He hugs me again. "Nothing to thank me for little brother. I love you."

"I love you, too." I think that might be the first time I've ever said those words to him, even though I've always felt them.

"We'll talk more tomorrow," he says meaningfully, and I know he's going to try to talk me out of going with Dad.

"Yeah," I say. "We'll talk."

Chapter Forty-Nine

Virginia

As soon as I roll over in bed, I realize I'm not in my own. My eyes pop open, the night before flooding over me like waves while I'm lost in the middle of the ocean.

Mom and Amelia.

Samantha, and what she said to me all those years ago.

Ryder, and how he held me, and listened, with no judgment.

It's still all too much.

Sitting up, I see a blanket and a big lump on the floor beside the bed. It only takes me a second to realize its Ryder. He slept on the floor next to me last night. Giving me space.

Instinct takes over and I crawl down on the floor beside him. When I push his hair back from his face, his eyes slowly open. "Thank you."

"For what?" He squints, obviously still tired, and then says, "I called your dad last night. I'm sorry if you're pissed, but I didn't want him to worry."

If anything, it makes me fall in love with him more. "For that. It's one of the things at least."

I thread my fingers through his and then Ryder holds our hands up. The light from his window highlights our hands. We both stare at them, Ryder twisting and turning our hands as though he's never seen them together before. It's the most incredible thing I've ever seen.

"My dad came to see me…"

My heart skips a few beats. "What? When?"

Ryder still watches our hands with the window as a backdrop. "Yesterday. He gave me a bus ticket to go out to where he's staying."

Now my heart has taken up residence in my throat. "Are you going?" The question hurts.

"I was going to…my bag is already packed. I just… I always felt like the only person who really loved me was him. Like he was the only one who saw something worthy in me. And then I fell for you, but after the party and everything, I didn't know what was going to happen. Which is bullshit in a way. It's all an excuse."

Tell me! I want to yell at him. *Are you going to go?* I need to know. My breath feels trapped in my lungs, scared to come out, but I fight it off, letting him speak.

"Then you came last night, and told me everything about your mom. I know you've never told anyone any of that. I was thinking about your mom and how her life was kind of decided by people who hurt her. No, that's not right. But they altered her life without her permission, which then altered yours. Luke and I talked after that, and…"

Ryder shrugs. "I always thought he saw me as a loser, the same way he saw Dad. He doesn't, though… He looked up to me. Wanted to protect me. He would have come back for me, and…"

He rolls over, onto his stomach, leaning on his arms. "Write a story with me, Virginia."

Finally, I breathe. "What?"

"I don't know shit about writing, but write a story with me. Our story. Your story. Mine. Whatever. Let's not be afraid to write our own. To decide who we want to be, who we already are."

I get what he's saying. We don't know much about life. Who really does? We all see things one way when most of the time, it's the complete opposite. Even when you live in the situation, if it's not yours, you don't get it. Maybe even if it *is* yours, you don't get it, but that doesn't mean we should be afraid to write our own stories. To live.

"My dad…" I say.

"We'll work around it. Or we won't, but at least we tried. At least we didn't give in." Ryder closes his eyes, and I miss the colors in them. "I don't want to steal cars, V. I don't want my dad to decide who I am."

Each of his words are a hand, a hand reaching out to me, reaching into my pockets, one by one, removing the rocks. Or maybe they're my hands, and maybe his words just show me it's okay to be the one to decide. Not to have to mold and shape and pretend to be anything. To be okay with who I am, flaws and all, and that ultimately, it's all up to me.

"I don't want my destiny decided for me…"

"It's not," he says.

"I like to write," I admit. "It's not what I want to do, but I'm good at it."

"I don't know what I'm good at yet, but I know there's something."

And then he kisses me, and I kiss him back. His body rests on mine, and I feel every inch of him. Feel that he wants me just as much as I want him, that it's okay not to be in a hurry. Our time will come. Soon.

I drop my head backward and Ryder kisses my throat.

"I know there's something for you, too," I tell him.

It's then I realize that's it's okay. Maybe I don't have to have all the answers. It's okay not to know what to do sometimes. It's okay to make things up as you go. That's kind of what Ryder and I did with each other—just made things up as we went along. And I think maybe ours might be the greatest story ever written.

Chapter Fifty

Ryder

I don't use the bus ticket but I go on a road trip all the same. As soon as Virginia leaves, Luke and I jump in his car, fill it up with gas, and hope like hell it will make it to Detroit and back.

His work wasn't too happy that he's taking a few days off, but it doesn't stop him. This is our time. The Blackstock brothers.

We basically eat nothing but gas station food the whole trip because it's cheap. We sleep in the car at rest stops or just keep driving, taking turns. It's even better than our day at the park when I was a kid. It's our adventure, the first one we've gone on together as a team.

Not Luke who is better than me, or Ryder who wants to be just like Dad.

Just…brothers.

The drive takes us a few days and we go to the hotel where we're supposed to meet Dad.

There's a knock at the door exactly when he said he'd come.

I'm sitting on the bed, my heart trying to run away from me. Luke squeezes my shoulder and whispers, "We got this."

Not, *you got this*. Not, *I got this*. *We got this.*

And we do.

Pushing to my feet, I rub my palms on my jeans before walking to the door. I open it and Dad smiles at me. There's a pinch in my chest but I ignore it. I have to. No matter what, he's my dad; but I don't want his life.

He takes one step into the room and freezes when he sees Luke sitting there.

"What the fuck is going on here, Ryder?"

"We didn't turn you in." I close the door. "But I'm not staying, either."

"So, he did turn you against me. You little bastard!" Dad goes after Luke, who jumps to his feet. Before Luke can do anything stupid, I jump between them. My dad isn't someone you want to fuck with. I've seen him beat people. I've seen him hurt them. But I know he won't hurt me.

"Luke!" I reach for him but he shakes me off.

"Just listen to him, Dad. Shut up and listen to what he has to say." Luke holds his hands up as if to say he's good.

"I…" It comes out all wrong and I have to clear my throat. The weight is on my chest again, but it's a different kind. It's the weight that comes with saying goodbye. "I don't want to do this. I thought I did my whole life. I thought I wanted to be just like you, but…" I shrug. "I think the only thing I ever really wanted was for you to love me. You loved what I could do. You loved that I was good and quick and thought well on the spot. I pretended that was the same thing as loving me."

But it wasn't. Maybe Dad loves me and maybe he doesn't.

Maybe he loves Luke and maybe he doesn't. Maybe he never thought his parents loved him so he doesn't know how to show us.

Maybe we'll never know. Life is full of uncertainty. All you can do is keep going.

Dad shoves Luke away, who stumbles backward. He looks at my brother, fire in his eyes. "This is *you*. You did this." And then to me. "It's a waste, Ryder. The world will always shit on people like us. I thought you were strong enough to fight back. You shouldn't have come. Neither of you. Are you going to rat me out?"

My vision gets a little fuzzy. "No."

"You're both just like her. Just like your mother. You think you're too good. Don't fucking turn me in. If you do, I'll know it's you. I'm done with you both."

Dad turns and walks out of the room. It's the first time he's said something like that about Mom. Hell, I don't even remember her. I was a baby when she bailed. Maybe she did think she was too good. Maybe he chased her away. We'll never know, and I'm okay with that. I have my friends. My brother. Virginia. And one day, I'll know who I am, too. That's all that matters.

"Come on, Luke. Let's go home."

Chapter Fifty-One
Virginia

Mom hadn't been home when I came back. Dad says we all need some time before we discuss things. It takes me a couple days to be ready to talk, and then finally I know I am.

This time, it is my decision for the family to sit around the dining room table.

Mom looks nervous, her hands on the table, and she's looking down at them. Or maybe it's not nerves; maybe it's sadness.

Dad looks at me, gives me his kind smile, and it's the strength I need.

"I'm sorry, Mom. So sorry. I didn't know….I didn't…" I shake my head. "Not knowing isn't an excuse. I wasn't fair to you, and I'm sorry about that."

Relief flashes across Mom's face, fear I hadn't realized was there disappearing. And it hurts…makes me feel incredible, but it hurts at the same time. She loves me so much that she can forgive the fact that I've been horrible to her for years, this quickly. "Oh honey. You're a child. You didn't know any better. You've been hurt. You were protecting your heart. How can I fault you for that?"

My body gets jittery. "I love you. I'm so sorry," I mumble again. I can't sit over here anymore so I push to my feet and go to her. I climb on her lap like I used to do when she read my stories as I kid. I wrap my arms around her neck and cry.

Cry for our family and what's it's been through.

Cry for Mom and the pain she lives with daily.

Cry for Grandma and her destiny.

Maybe I even cry for Virginia Woolf, too. The mind is a funny thing. It's not always something we can control, or even something that makes sense. It's hard sometimes to see through the fog, the pain, hurt, fear and everything else we live with every day. Virginia Woolf couldn't do it. Annette Klinger couldn't, either. My heart breaks for them—that they couldn't get the help they needed for a disease they couldn't control.

Mom is fighting for that.

And I will as well.

"I think...I think I'd like to go. Talk to someone with you. Understand what's going on with you better and maybe even...maybe even understand some things about myself."

Dad sits across the table from us as we hug. Hug and cry. His girls. That's what he used to call us. Even after they separated, he called us his girls.

Finally the tears stop. "Maybe I can start coming to your house on the weekends sometimes. I'd like to start staying there again."

"I would love that, Virginia. So much."

Mom lets me go and I sit beside her, instead of moving back to my chair next to Dad. "I want to talk about Ryder." My parents share a look and I forge on. "He's a good guy. He's trying to be more than what he thought was his destiny. He loves me and I love him, and—"

"And you can see him," Dad finishes.

"What?" I'd been prepared to go into the whole *I turn
eighteen in a couple months* thing, but it looks like I won't have
to.

"He called me when you went there, Lulu. He didn't have to
do that. I'm not going to pretend I'm not still angry, but your
mom reminded me what it's like to be young. And that boy
would do anything to protect you. That much is obvious."

"There will be rules," Mom adds.

"Yeah. Sure. Anything."

Both my parents laugh and I'm glad we're like this—the
abnormal family that still loves each other and gets along, even
when a marriage ends.

"No more drinking, or drugs, and he needs to come around
the house."

I don't tell Dad he's here often, just not when he's home.

"Your mom needs to meet him as well, and school still needs
to come first. You can't—"

"We do homework together. Every day. He's trying to bring
his grades up."

Dad nods and smiles. "Good. That's good."

We all go into the kitchen together to make dinner. My
parents laugh and tease each other. They laugh and tease me. I
wonder if Ryder and I will be like them one day. Hopefully still
together, yet I want the respect and love between us that my
parents have. It's so thick around them, it touches me every time
we're together.

That's life, I think. Sometimes people who love each other

and are perfect for each other don't work out. Sometimes the person who should be all wrong for you couldn't be more right.

Life never goes the direction you think it will. No one's destiny is mapped out for them. Life is full of choices and happiness and heartbreak. And I wouldn't have it any other way.

Epilogue

There once was a girl named Virginia. She had hair made of honey and a life made of dreams. It wasn't Perfect, no one's was. But it was her life, and she loved it.

It wasn't always like that, and that too, is life. It starts one way and ends another, because there isn't life without growth.

When she was seventeen years old, she realized what growth really was. What life really was.

We are all people named Fear.

Perfect.

Liar.

Want.

Lonely.

Guilt.

Control.

Fate.

Hate.

Denial.

Thief.

Sadness.

Reckless.

Love.

We're also all more than that. It's all those identities that make us human. It's all those people who show us we're alive.

And she wanted to live.

The End

Keep reading for a letter from the author.

Dear Reader,

In high school I did my Jr. Research Paper on DID, though at the time it was more often called MPD—Multiple Personality Disorder. I did it because I wanted to learn more about the disease that a close family friend of ours suffered from. I've seen the hardships DID, and mental illness can cause families. There is a ripple effect, and each and every person deals with it differently. The way Virginia dealt won't be the same way others do but her journey was true to her.

For those of you out there who suffer from mental illness know that you aren't alone. And that it's okay. Reach out for help and you are strong. You. Are. Strong.

And to our friend wherever you are, I hope you are well. Thanks for being so open and honest with me about your struggles all those years ago.

Nyrae

Acknowledgement

As always my family comes first. Thank you for dealing with me. I know I'm not always easy and when I get into my zone I sometimes block out everything else. I'm sorry for that and I love you. I couldn't do it without you.

My readers. There aren't enough words to thank you for supporting me. For taking this journey with me. There have been a lot of hard times. A lot. Most happen behind the scenes and what gets me through those times is you. Writing stories that I hope you will love. Thank you, thank you, thank you from the bottom of my heart for giving your time to me and my characters.

Thanks to Wendy Higgins, who is my first reader and my best friend. Love you! Also to Steph Campbell, Kelley York and Jolene Perry for always listening, even if you're silently shaking your head at me. LOL. I couldn't do this without you, my friends. I'm so lucky to have you! Hugs and love to you.

David James, Jamie Manning, Heather Young-Nichols, Sarah Arthur, Momo, Tricia, Melissa, and I'm so scared I am missing someone. If I am, I'm so sorry! But thank you all for reading and helping me get this story into shape.

I am so lucky to be surrounded by such smart, cool people.

Books two and three of the Misfits series available in 2015.

About The Author

Writing has always been Nyrae Dawn's passion. Even when she was too busy chasing kids or working, writing stories was never far from her mind.

Nyrae gravitates toward character-driven stories. Whether reading or writing, she loves emotional journeys. It's icing on the cake when she really *feels* something, but is able to laugh too. She's also a proud romantic at heart who has a soft spot for flawed characters. She loves people who aren't perfect, who make mistakes but also have big hearts.

Nyrae resides in sunny Southern California with her husband (who still makes her swoon) and her two awesome kids. When she's not with her family, you can be pretty sure you'll find her with a book in her hand or her laptop and an open document in front of her.

She writes for Entangled Publishing, Grand Central Publishing and is self-published.

Nyrae is represented by Jane Dystel of Dystel and Goderich Literary Management.

https://www.facebook.com/nyraedawnwrites

https://twitter.com/NyraeDawn

www.nyraedawn.blogspot.com